M000312328

2nd SIGHT

Capturing Insight

By Ben A. Sharpton

2ⁿᵈ SIGHT

Limitless Publishing, LLC
Kailua, HI 96734
www.limitlesspublishing.com

Formatting: Limitless Publishing

ISBN-13: 978-1-68058-679-4
ISBN-10: 1-68058-679-3

DEDICATION

To Nikki and Jonny

Embrace Your Dreams
Understand Through insight
Lead With Vision And Compassion

"Your old men will dream dreams, and your young men will see visions."
—Ancient Prophesy

CHAPTER ONE

The body was heavy.

He dragged the corpse through the kitchen and into the attached garage. Sweat poured from his balding forehead down to his glistening nose where wire frame glasses threatened to slide down to his steely goatee. He paused to push the glasses up higher on his nose, only to have them slide down again.

The legs of the body bounced three times down the garage steps and then slid across the cement floor with a swoosh as the man dragged it to the rear of the car. He dropped the shoulders, which bounced along with the bloody head, on the floor. Sticking his hand into his pocket, he found the key fob and pressed the tiny button to unlock the trunk. Sucking in a lung-full of fresh air, he hefted the body, first the upper torso and then the legs, and rolled them all into the trunk. Blood oozed from the head onto the carpet. He'd have to clean it up and then trade the car for a new one to hide any evidence of his presence. Fake IDs would add another layer of anonymity between him and the body, now crumpled into somewhat of a fetal position. "How ironic," he said to the body.

After closing the trunk, he leaned back against it and assessed his situation.

The project failed. A lifetime of work disappeared as if caught up in a roaring fire. The opportunity to make a name for himself and change the world was gone.

The man in the trunk had given up just when things were finally coming together. He wasn't committed. He was too weak. The man had failed.

But there was another.

***

Scott entered the break room in a bit of a daze. His cup was empty and he needed another shot before returning to an office full of spreadsheets, requisitions, and unread emails. Running his fingers through his thick blond hair he wondered how long he would keep it, given the stress of his job.

The room began to fade like images at the end of a movie and he went down like a sandbag. His head bashed on the tile floor as his eyesight slipped out of focus.

One of the custodians, an older lady he had bumped into as he hustled down the hall, called from the doorway. "Mr. Moore. Mr. Moore. Are you all right?"

Another custodian, dressed in a crisp, clean uniform, stood beside her in shock. Scott had not seen her before but he did notice a slight bump in her belly.

He heard a radio playing '70s music. He was in a car, flying down a two-lane road. Rain fell and the road was slick. He was behind the wheel and in control of the car. Sorta. The wipers clunked back and forth, leaving watery streaks on the windshield, blurring the road ahead.

Looking down at his hands, he was surprised to see his fingernails were covered with nail polish. This is freakin' weird. The image and sounds faded in and out and the radio blared some song about the prolific presence of signs in our world.

A pickup truck barreled down a side road heading toward him. He pounded the brake with his right foot and then with both feet, trying to slow down. The pickup—a Chevy?—bolted through the stop sign just as he hit the intersection sliding sideways. He screamed, except it didn't sound like his voice. It was a woman's voice—high pitched. He wasn't wearing a seatbelt. He felt, actually felt, his chest slam into the steering wheel and heard tires squealing and metal scraping, bending, collapsing. The car spun around like a skateboarder doing a ten-eighty. It slammed again into the side of the speeding vehicle and Scott was thrown against the door, cracking glass with his head, and slamming his left ankle against the brake pedal, and then against the firewall. Something crunched. He wasn't sure if it was metal, or ankle, or both.

He leaned right and braced himself as hard as he could against another side assault. He bounced off the passenger door like a basketball, hurtling in

3

the opposite direction.

The hallucination faded in and out. Just before blacking out again he watched the custodian running toward him. He realized he had never noticed she walked with a limp.

Lying on rough, rocky asphalt facing the car, he studied the wreckage. The car was twisted and mangled like those strips of metal left behind after opening a can of sardines. His hip hurt like hell. He raised his head a bit, feeling a jolt of pain, and chanced a look into the gleaming hubcap. In its reflection he saw his body, bloody and disheveled. The face on the body wasn't his but that of the custodian.

The hazy image faded and a new one took its place.

He was in a strange place, a big park. Dogs were running around in a fenced-in area.

The image seemed to slip in and out.

He was sitting on a park bench opposite a pregnant lady who sat on another park bench. He was talking with her, but Scott didn't really understand it...Something about teaching in a University.

A systems analyst who had been reading a USA Today in the break room reached him first and started shaking his shoulder. "Wake up, Mr. Moore. Wake up."

Scott came to again, surrounded by a small crowd of Bell Intelliservices employees. A security guard was there. So were a handful of front-liners. He shook off their concerns. "It's okay, guys," he said. "I just tripped. Probably stepped on my own shoelaces." Looking down at his feet, he noticed both shoes were laced up, so he quickly bent over to untie and retie the lace on his right shoe.

A security guard helped him stand to his feet. "You need to see a doctor," he said.

"No. Really. This happens all the time," Scott said. "I'm just clumsy." With that he stumbled out into the hallway and toward the front doors. "I'll head home a little early today and get some rest. See you all tomorrow."

Scott hated these seizures. Strange images, indiscernible and unpredictable, embarrassed him over and over. They had started when he was younger and seemed to be coming more often now. And, they were more intense.

"You're in no shape to drive," the security guard called. "Let us get you a cab."

Scott shook his head and waved goodbye on his way to the lobby and through the huge glass doors. He could feel their stares piercing his back as he headed for his car in the parking lot. He'd go home and rest a bit before Grace got off work.

Tomorrow was going to be a tough day.

***

It would be a shitty day, maybe one of the shittiest. Scott pulled his Toyota Prius into the employee parking lot of the small inbound call center where he had worked for eight years. All of the five hundred souls who worked at this facility knew this particular day would come, but few knew when. Scott did.

Housed in a long, low prefabricated building thrown up at the start of the internet boom in the late '90s, Bell Intelliservices provided incoming telephone customer service to about a dozen American businesses. Inside, hundreds of employees sat in rows upon rows of cubicles, answering phones methodically, efficiently, and professionally. Many similar organizations off-shored their inbound service centers to other countries, in particular, India and Colombia, where operators used names like Kevin and Mary in an effort to fool American callers into overlooking their thick accents. Others had outsourced to individuals working out of their homes using their own computers and telephone equipment. Bell, however, had hung onto the more traditional model and was no longer competitive. For several months executives at Bell made plans to make the company leaner in order to stay in business.

Leaner meant layoffs. At Bell, if headcount needed to be slashed, Scott Moore became the serial slasher.

His To Do List on this day included giving eighteen middle managers their walking papers. Someone else in Human Resources would oversee group layoffs of another hundred frontline employees. Chances were this would not be the last downsizing this year.

Performing such events—his boss called them "reducing our footprint"—was one of the worst aspects of Human Resources. Poor suckers in that department had to deliver the news of one of the most heart-rending experiences an employee might ever face and chances are a few of the human resource employees would be the first to go. Some executives at a much higher level in the organization decided to cut out-of-control expenses, often out of control because of reckless spending by those executives. They always cut labor costs. Layoffs were part of the insane binge-and-purge mentality of business executives who saw employees as more of a commodity than an asset. Scott hated such mass firings more than root canals, political corruption, and marital infidelity combined.

He climbed the steps to the front of the two story office building, entered the lobby, nodded to the receptionist who returned his greeting with a concerned frown as she had every day since the rumors began three months earlier, and right-turned down the hall to his office. He fished a key chain from his pocket and unlocked his office door, set his briefcase beneath his desk, and returned to the hall to fetch a large cup of hot, black coffee. Within ten minutes he had filled his cup, greeted his assistant, smiled at several office clerks, listened as a nasal-voiced recruiter complained about a supervisor's treatment of her employees, and stepped into the office of Kathy Becker, Director of Human

Resources.

Kathy's office was a little larger than Scott's, but the decor, the furniture, and the lighting were identical. Of course, Kathy had a bigger office chair. "Ready for this?" she asked, handing him a stack of beige folders containing severance papers. She was a rather large lady who wore flowing flowery dresses that draped around her office chair like a judge's robes. Scott had often thought the larger chair might not have been a director's perk but a simple necessity.

"No," he replied, but the two proceeded anyway. They confirmed the names of the managers and directors on his list. Kathy encouraged him with a smile and the phrase, "I really don't like 'redundancy eliminations'—new catchphrase—But, it's the best thing for the company, Scott."

"I know," he responded.

He returned to his desk, laid the folders out before him, picked up his phone, and dialed Anderson, Joy's extension to ask her to come to his office. Flicking the button on his ballpoint pen, he waited for Joy to answer. The clicking rhythm was somehow soothing. Stealing a moment, he glanced at the framed portrait of he and Grace and Gumby taken on his thirty-fifth birthday. It centered him.

The shitty day began.

At lunch, Scott downed a ham sandwich and chips from vending machines in the HR break room. He never liked eating this way, but he had too much to do on this day.

At two forty-five he returned to Kathy's office.

She spun around in her large chair. "How'd it

go?" Her cheeks bulged when she smiled.

"Tough." He handed the file folder to her. "Helen Watson is out sick today. Otherwise, I worked through the rest on the list without incident. Security has the swipe cards. Most of them handled it like professionals."

"Good job," she said, taking the folders from him. She swiveled her hefty frame around and retrieved another folder from the credenza behind her. Spinning back around she rested fleshy arms on her desk, sighed in an almost sincere manner, and looked into his eyes. "This is for you."

The punch to his stomach knocked the air out of him. He noticed his hands trembled as he took the folder. Sweat dripped from his armpits staining his blue shirt. Shit. That was all that came to mind.

"This is so hard for me to do," she said.

But she had no idea. He opened the folder, but the words and columns blurred together. He had given his best years to the company, working endless hours through countless weeks, to keep it afloat and productive, and the company repaid his hard work by dumping him like a diseased piece of meat. Betrayal was a bitch. Kathy was a bitch. Bell was a bitch.

"The severance is never enough, but it is more generous than that of some of our competitors."

He had uttered the same words seventeen times that day. He looked up from the folder and saw her lips moving but heard nothing she said. Eight years with the call center, moving up from human resources supervisor to manager to assistant director, suppressing potential walkouts, heading off two union attempts, and a lawsuit to ultimately get axed. Shit, again.

"If you'd like to come in this weekend to collect your things, that might be easier."

"Huh?"

"Just call me when you're ready and I'll make arrangements with security," her lips said.

Kathy didn't even have the balls to meet him when he came in for his belongings. No surprise there. He looked back at the blurry paper.

"You'll land on your feet in no time," she said, as he had said countless times before. She offered the same fat-cheeked smile and reached out to shake his hand.

Scott walked down the hall, past the receptionist's desk in the lobby where he assumed she still smiled uncomfortably and through the front doors for one of his final times. Stunned by the day's events, the blinding late afternoon sun only heightened his confusion. He stumbled down the front steps and into the parking lot. His hands dripped sweat, making his briefcase difficult to hold. His head ached like an infected wound.

"How could you do this to me?" Frank Johnson, a five-year veteran waited by Scott's Prius. "Why did you pick me?" His clip-on tie was gone and his shirttail hung out of his pants, giving him a ragged, I-don't-give-a-damn look. His glaring eyes would scare the eminent psychiatrist, Carl Jung.

"Frank," Scott answered, holding up his hand and shaking his head. "It's nothing personal. The company downsized." He didn't mention he was part of the down-sizing.

"What am I gonna do now? I'm sixty-one years old. Who would want to hire me?" A tart, pungent smell of whiskey floated from Frank to Scott in the hot afternoon breeze.

Scott felt thirsty.

He looked up through exhausted eyes into the face of someone worse off than himself. He searched his aching mind for the right calculated response, but came up with zeroes. "I don't know, Frank." Like a glaring spotlight the afternoon sun burned down mercilessly.

Frank's eyes began to flood. He wiped the back of his hand across a sweaty lip.

"Look, Frank," Scott said. "Take a couple of days off and then go through the outplacement program. You'll be amazed at how helpful those guys can be." He tried to make his voice sound convincing. It didn't work. He and Frank knew it was bullshit.

Frank's hands shook. "Brittany's pregnant," he whispered. "My daughter's pregnant and she ain't got nowhere to go." The shaking moved from his hands to his shoulders.

"Ohhh, crap," Scott muttered. He wanted to say he knew how Frank felt, but since he had no children himself it would be a lie. Ignoring his human resources training not to physically touch employees, he reached a hand out and pulled Frank into a man hug to calm him. "Certainly the severance pay, the extended insurance…"

"He left her," Frank blubbered through muffled tears. "That no-good boyfriend of hers left after he knocked her up. I've gotta cover three mouths, and hospital expenses, now. I already have a second mortgage on the house. There's nothin' else I can do."

"Something will come along, Frank. You'll see." But Scott didn't believe it. Obviously, Frank didn't either. He pulled away, shook his head and shuffled, defeated, to his aging truck in the back of the lot, his shoes sounding like sandpaper on the asphalt.

A hot breeze blew across the lot and Scott longed for his auto air conditioning. Leaning against his car, he watched as the beaten man drove away. He reached down to the door handle but lacked the energy to pull it open. He leaned again against the hot metal of the automobile. Finally, breathing in deeply, he pulled back and dragged the handle up. The door opened. It took Scott just about as much energy to climb into the driver's seat and start the car.

He backed up silently, adjusted the transmission, and slid out of the parking lot, past a black BMW parked near the entrance.

It had been a shitty day.

CHAPTER TWO

Gumby jumped off the bed and charged the back door as Scott's Prius slid silently into the garage. He never expected anyone to come home this early but he always welcomed Scott or Grace or the mailman or burglars or anyone else to their house. He wiggled his butt as much as possible as if to make up for the small nub of a tail that boxers have after the vet births them and whacks it off. When excited he tended to knock over small chairs, briefcases, floor lamps, toddlers—anything within eighteen inches of the floor and in the path of his shaking torso, so Scott did all he could to calm the wriggling beast.

Gumby made Scott smile. The expression surprised him because he realized he hadn't smiled since walking into his office that morning. He seldom smiled these days. He had little to smile about. Now he had less. He dug a treat from the canister on the kitchen counter and tossed it in the direction of the excited dog, who snatched the gift mid-air, swallowed it in one sudden motion, and stood dead still staring at him, waiting for another.

It was just after four o'clock, and Grace wouldn't be home from the hospital for two or three more hours. An ache pounded his head like a base drum. He grabbed a bottle of Jack Daniels and filled a glass with the golden liquid. Gulping several swallows, he felt it burn its way down, sanitizing the day's pain and grief, and filling his mind with a numbing sense of nothingness.

Scott yanked open the sliding glass door and glared through the back porch into the yard, drink in hand. Recent winds had broken a rather large limb on the old oak tree and it swayed precariously toward his porch roof. He'd tend to it another day—certainly had time to do so now. He sucked down several more therapeutically scorching swallows of whiskey and stepped out onto the porch. Checking the settings on the hot tub, he cranked the jets up high and stood his half empty glass on a nearby wooden table.

Balance was beginning to be a challenge, but he held onto the edge of the tub while he tugged off his tie, shirt, and trousers. He kicked his shoes back toward the glass door bouncing one off the porch ceiling, ripped off his socks and, dressed only in his boxer-briefs, leaned over and rolled himself into the hot tub with a splash. Entry into the water was messier than he had expected, with the scorching liquid splashing back and forth in little tidal waves. It rushed over the edges, drained down the side of the tub, and soaked the floor where Gumby feverishly lapped up as much of the puddled water as he could. Scott lay back into the soothing hot water and watched the ceiling fan circling overhead like blades on a helicopter moments before liftoff…or crash. Eventually, the soothing Jacuzzi jets and the ceiling fan and the Jack Daniels worked together to lull Scott into a mild and welcome trance.

He heard laughter and music. Kathy Becker, dressed somewhat like a glamorous Christmas tree, stood behind a small podium, and said something about how happy she was to receive the prestigious Bell award. Someone in the room yelled, "And the bonus that goes with it." Applause erupted from the crowd led by Bill Bell, the CEO. She turned and waved at everyone in attendance, grinned her pudgy grin and then darkness covered her face and the stage and the hall.

In a flash, the image changed.

The darkness was bleak. He heard the sound of movement. Footsteps. Someone was walking through the house. Drawers slid open on plastic rollers and something heavy was extracted, somewhat noisily, from inside. He smelled a wood fireplace. Smoke. His vision was impaired—not unfocused as much as just blurry. Too bright, here. Too dark, there. He realized he wasn't in his own house. It frightened him because he had no idea whose it was. He'd never been there before. He looked down and saw his shoes walking, except they weren't his shoes. He never wore brown boots. He didn't own a rug like the one beneath his feet.

He raised his right hand with some difficulty and beheld a pistol. He turned his wrist first right and then left and examined the metallic weapon. He couldn't name the brand or the style—he knew nothing about guns—and he couldn't understand why he held this one.

Scott felt his body fall backwards only to flop into a lounge chair. Cloth upholstery, not leather like the one in his living room, surrounded him. His feet raised and his head dropped into a reclining position.

He searched the house for an indication of his whereabouts. The newspaper was too far away to read the heading, but he assumed it was the local paper. Something, maybe magazines, were stacked on a nearby table, but they were face down. He couldn't read the titles or tell the dates. The smoky smell changed, morphed, became clearer. It smelled like cigarette smoke. Scott didn't smoke cigarettes. Turning his head more to the right he saw a picture frame containing a photo of a man holding the hand of an elderly lady in a hospital bed, her eyes barely open, almost lifeless. He stared at the photo for a long, long time, unable to recognize the woman. But the man looked familiar, like Frank Johnson. The frame brightened and then darkened.

Then he saw the pistol rise up and slide into his mouth. He tasted the bitter metal and smelled the distinct gun powder odor.

His world exploded.

Scott scrambled out of the hot tub and flung himself over the edge screaming, "No, no, no!" A flash of pain jolted his knee when it banged against the concrete floor. Late afternoon sun shone through the screened windows and the ceiling fan clacked noisily overhead.

Gumby raced back onto the porch eager to be a part of whatever happened out there.

Scott dragged himself to the door, trembling. "No, no, no," as Gumby licked the water off his shoulders and neck.

And Grace was there. She grabbed something dry and warm and wrapped it around Scott's shoulders, pulling him close to her blue nurse's scrubs. "Scott," she said aloud, trying to be heard over his own cries. "It's okay. I'm here, now." She pulled him closer.

He lay his head against her breast and gulped down deep breaths of calming air while the headaches came in waves. He shivered so hard he kicked over one of Grace's flower pots, spilling black dirt and violets and little white granules of something used to retain water. The action scared Gumby so bad that the dog ran back inside the house.

"Did you see something?" Grace asked.

"Yeah."

"I'm sorry I wasn't here."

"You can't always be here."

"I try."

**

In October of his freshman year of college, just when he had been drowning in tests and textbooks and thought he couldn't manage anything else, Scott met Grace.

But Julie came before Grace. The co-ed had befriended him the first day he arrived on campus. Scott had no idea why they became friends. They had very little in common. Both were incoming freshman but she was much more organized than he. He struggled with grades. She excelled. He was straight as an arrow. She was "curious." He was healthy and fit. She was wheelchair-bound.

They met in the student center when he tripped over her. Consumed with confusion and personal doubts, Scott had forgotten about his Philosophy 101 course and jumped up to sprint to the Waldrop building. Julie was sitting at a table behind him and he barreled over her like a halfback diving for the goal line.

"Shit!" She shuffled the two big wheels to gain stability.

"Sorry," Scott exclaimed, reaching for books and papers scattered across the slick tile floor. "Personal emergency."

"Restrooms are over there, Slick," she said pointing down the hall.

Scott sized her up. Her stocky form seemed developed from years of pushing the wheels on her chair. Her dark hair swept across her forehead as if a skilled painter had placed it there. Her eyes sparkled as only attractive people's eyes sparkle and her radiant smile lifted the world.

"Sorry."

"Late for class?"

"Yeah," he said, scanning his watch. "Damn. It's

half over."

"Then pull up a chair, Bud. You're too late to learn anything now."

Scott hesitated, then complied. Laying his books and papers on the table, he slid into the empty chair next to her. They chatted about everything unimportant, like majors, classes, campus life and more.

"What's with the chair?" Scott asked, curious and feeling more relaxed. Then he realized how derogatory it sounded and started to backpedal.

Julie stopped smiling and stared him down as if trying to determine whether he was ready for what she was about to say. She looked down at the chair and then back up to Scott. At first he thought she was playing some stupid stare-down game but her answer snapped him back to reality. "I have Congenital Muscular Dystrophy—CMD."

Scott had heard the term, "Muscular Dystrophy," and remembered seeing pictures of shriveled and deformed children, but he didn't realize there were different types of the illness. In fact, he knew nothing about CMD. "How long?"

Julie took in a deep breath and closed her eyes as if to stop herself from throwing her books at him. "All my life," she said, glaring. "That's what 'congenital' means."

"Oh." He felt stupid. "Sorry."

She shook her head. "It is what it is, you know?"

He tilted his head to the left, trying to understand how someone with such a deadly illness could be so flippant about it.

And that's how it began. Their friendship grew.

Scott was never attracted to Julie romantically. Their attraction wasn't based on sympathy. He never felt sorry for Julie because she was in a wheelchair. In fact, after a while her chair seemed like a part of her, like a tiller might be an extension of a sailor out on the ocean.

Instead, as corny as it might sound, Scott thought of her as a light in a forest, water in a dessert, a welcome haven in the middle of a storm, a friend when a friend was most needed. She was there. With him. Unconditionally.

They eventually talked about his seizures which never seemed to bother her. She accepted his shyness with grace, like a welcome mat. Anything Scott considered to be a personality deficiency, Julie accepted without question. They were friends.

And that was enough.

Then he met Grace.

Julie had been walking, or rolling, in her case, across the quad in the middle of the day. Beside her an attractive coed, arms loaded with books, was trying to keep up. She wasn't a knockout, but neither was she a skag. She could make a guy proud to take her home to meet his parents.

Julie waved him over as soon as she saw him. "Hey, Scotty," she said, using her own pet name for him. "Meet my roommate, Grace."

She smiled. He smiled back and nodded. She carried her alluring frame with a confidence seldom seen on campus. He felt clumsy and inadequate. He left his fears behind and moved closer to meet her.

"Grace is a nursing student—a sophomore."

"Oh," he said. Most incoming freshmen roomed

with other incoming freshmen. Grace and Julie's situation was a little unusual.

"Yeah, my freshman roommate found somebody else," she spoke for the first time. "She claimed she couldn't live with me 'cause I was too demanding."

"Now you know why we get along," Julie said with a wink.

"If you ask me," Grace continued, "I'm not demanding. I just know what I want and I set out to get it."

At first, her confidence set Scott back a bit. But, it also appealed to his competitive side and he felt she could be someone special. After all, if she and Julie could hit it off, perhaps she and Scott could, as well.

They did. It was almost as if they had never not been friends. In her own somewhat commanding style, Grace helped Scott get his shit together, offering tips on study habits, and showing him the ropes. The more they stayed together, the more Scott enjoyed her confident style, compassionate eyes, and directive behavior.

One night, watching a campus movie-on-the-lawn, sitting on the grass between Julie in her chair and Scott splayed out feet first on the lawn, Grace slid her hand over his. It was a warm, bold gesture, inviting and somewhat enticing.

Scott, surprised at first and intrigued next, turned his hand over to allow their fingers to intertwine and struggled to keep his glowing smile from being too obvious. After all, he didn't want to chase her away.

Later, Grace stayed behind after Julie strolled to

her dorm. She walked with Scott through the grassy quad beneath an umbrella of majestic oaks. She talked about her interest in helping people and how a nursing career could make that happen. This seemed like a perfect fit to Scott and he countered, describing his own interest in human resources. The night held a fresh breeze filling and fulfilling him. Beneath a campus light they shared a warm and welcome kiss.

Scott wanted to invite Grace to his room, but he knew his nerdy roommate would have his nose stuck in a book and would refuse to give them the space they needed. Besides, such a move might be a little too soon.

They parted and Scott returned to his own room feeling all was right with a world that often seemed as black as night.

Sorta.

***

Winter had followed fall and chased after spring and Grace and Scott grew together as lovers. They made time to share almost every free minute together and enjoyed the heck out of college life.

One night, soon after they met, Scott brought his guitar to the quad and serenaded Grace as best he could, despite an out-of-tune guitar and out-of-tune voice. She seemed to love it, leaning back against an old, grand tree and drinking in the music like a thirsty traveler in a vast dessert. Scott enjoyed the time so much he serenaded her every night afterwards for a month.

In March, just before sunrise, exhausted from midterms and passionate love making with Grace, Scott returned to his room late at night and fell onto his bed, clothes and all. His head had just connected with the pillow when he was out cold. That's when the hallucinations came again.

A foggy and blurry image revealed a wheelchair carrying a passenger who looked a lot like Julie.

She rolled down a campus sidewalk. Grace's voice suggested they grab some coffee. Ahead, a crosswalk led to a row of shops on the other side of the street. A glance to the right showed the Zombie Coffee Shop, one of their favorite haunts. The potent aroma of coffee floated to him and then changed to the smell of wet socks which were pervasive in his dorm room.

The scene shifted and faded as sunlight slipped in and out of overhead clouds. Scott recognized Grace's voice as the one who was talking with Julie.

"So, what's new?"

"That geek in Spanish has hit on me no less than four times this week," Julie said.

The image faded out again.

"…kinda cute, you know."

"I think he has a fetish for paraplegics." Both girls laughed.

"Sounds like more fun than most of the losers on campus." Julie looked back over her shoulder and

laughed. A group of three girls, giggling and laughing but not paying attention, appeared in his path. One bumped into him, forcing him to spin away from Julie for just a moment.

The image faded again and Scott heard a noise that sounded like the squeal of tires followed by a bone-grinding crash. The image came back into focus.

Julie lay in the road in a broken heap. Parts of her body were scraped and mutilated and blood splattered the bricks beneath her. He screamed and ran into the street.

Scott sat up, awake. His pillow was soaked with sweat. The image scorched the backs of his eyes as if he had stared into the blazing sun. He jumped out of bed, knocking over a chair and a stack of books, and dashed out of his room and down the hall and out of the dorm.

Within seconds he was charging across the campus, heading for the bank of shops on the other side. The crosswalk was empty. Students moved here and there without incident, chatting and laughing and heading to or from class.

Scott ran to the Zombie Coffee Shop but the outside glare prevented him from seeing inside. Cupping his hands over his eyes he pressed his face against the window. Neither Grace nor Julie were there. Bewildered, he backed away. The experience had seemed so real, so authentic, but was nothing more than just a fuzzy dream. A vivid, horrifying dream.

He had turned away like the creatures who shared a name with the coffee shop, and shuffled back toward his dorm.

***

Rain crashed on the roof and into the gutters, through downspouts and onto the lawn to settle in ever-growing puddles throughout the yard. Scott watched through the bay windows of his living room as Kathy Becker steered her Lexus RX450h through the downpour in his driveway and came to a stop just inches away from his garage door. She flung her door open, extended a purple umbrella, and cocked it like a shotgun until it expanded. She rocked her large rain-coated frame from the car into a standing position beneath the parasol, which caused the vehicle to rise up slightly as if to sigh in relief, and walked as fast as she could in high heels down the walkway in front of Scott's window and up his front steps. By the time her pudgy fingers pressed the doorbell, Scott had already opened the door.

"Hi, Kathy," he said as politely as he could manage. "Won't you come in?"

Gumby barked in the family room where Scott had sentenced him when her car pulled into the driveway. He loved welcoming visitors, all visitors, to their home. Those who knew Scott and Grace well saw Gumby as a playful puppy, simply acting out his own role in life. He scared the hell out of those who didn't understand. Kathy Becker wouldn't understand.

"Why, thank you, Scott," she said, setting her umbrella aside on his front porch. A puddle of water started to form around the tip.

He thanked the timing gods that Grace was at work. When she learned Scott had been fired, she wanted to personally help Kathy Becker empathize with the pain other employees felt after lay-offs. Had she been here this morning, she would surely have told Kathy where to store her umbrella.

He took her raincoat and hung it on a hook in the front closet. As he suspended the voluptuous overcoat, he noticed his hands were shaking. It was unusual for the boss who just fired you to show up in your living room.

"Would you like some coffee?" he asked, an effort toward politeness to the woman who had just laid him off. "I was about to pour myself a cup," he lied. He seldom drank the stuff when he didn't go into the office, but Kathy didn't know that.

"That sounds good," she said. "With cream and sugar, please," smiling in a pudgy way like a kid asking for an extra scoop of ice cream. "Two spoonfuls of sugar, please," she added.

Scott threw Gumby a chew treat and poured two cups, hers with cream and several spoonfuls of sugar. His, black. He returned to the living room where Kathy sat on the sofa, browsing a recent edition of a magazine.

"What brings you out on such a nasty day?" Scott asked, handing Kathy her cup. He hoped she had some questions about some paperwork, or about the last employee meeting or about where to find a stinking file on his stinking hard drive. He knew she wasn't visiting to invite him back to work.

"I've got terrible news," she said. She lowered her double-chin to her chest and looked at him with puppy dog eyes.

He took a deep breath wondering what might have happened. Did one of the supervisors file a lawsuit against the company on the way their dismissal was handled? Did some wacko call in a bomb threat? The irony of a disgruntled former employee making a telephone call to a telephone call center almost made him smile, but he suppressed it. He swallowed and awaited the bad news, whatever it was.

"Frank Johnson shot himself last night." She watched him like a seasoned hunter might watch a deer, observing his reaction.

Pain, guilt, fear knotted the pit of his stomach. Scott took a sip of coffee. "Is he all right?"

"No, he passed away before paramedics could arrive." She took a sip of her coffee. "You don't seem surprised."

Scott said, "I was afraid something like this might happen to Frank."

"What do you mean?"

Scott felt like he was being cross-examined. He knew Kathy's job was to obtain all the details so she could speak intelligently during the inevitable investigation. But he didn't like being interrogated.

"Frank was obviously upset about the layoffs. He has been under a lot of pressure since his wife died."

"Security said they saw you and Frank arguing in

the parking lot. Is that true?"

Scott shook his head. "We weren't arguing." He slurped the hot coffee, hoping a shot of caffeine would help him think.

Kathy took out a pad of paper and a pen. "Do you mind?"

Scott knew the routine. He shook his head. "Frank was standing by my car after you…when I left the building," he said. "He was obviously angry. He asked why we chose him and what he would do now, given his age and circumstances."

"Did you say anything to anger him?"

"Of course, not. I played it strictly by the book." Scott hated such questions, but knew she was just trying to cover her rather large ass. She was the queen of ass-covering.

"You were pretty upset yourself," she said in an insinuating tone.

He took a deep breath. "Given the circumstances, I'd say I handled the entire day quite professionally. I told him to go to the outplacement center. I said things would get better. I encouraged him. Nothing else." He stared at her, challenged her.

Kathy defended herself. "Understand that we're not suggesting that you did anything wrong."

"His daughter is pregnant," Scott said.

"I beg your pardon?"

"After his wife died, his daughter moved back in with him. Now, she's pregnant, and her boyfriend has skipped town. Frank told me he didn't know how he would make ends meet after losing his job. That's a lot of pressure dumped on one man in a very short amount of time."

"Oh."

"Layoffs have consequences," Scott said, allowing one little dig. It felt good.

"Yes, they do," Kathy said, standing as if to leave. Scott assumed she didn't want to give him time to dump his own complaints on her. "I'll have my assistant call you when I have information about the funeral."

"Thank you," Scott answered. "I want to be there." It was one of the last things he wanted to do. He felt too close to the situation. The funeral would bring back painful memories. He also dreaded seeing executives from Bell Intelliservices who would attend, ignorant of how hypocritical it might appear. He had nothing but contempt for those corporate assholes.

Kathy and Scott said their goodbyes, and he helped her drag on her soaking wet raincoat at the front door.

"You do understand that this is all about the business," she said, half asking.

"It always is," he said.

As she marched away in her high heeled shoes to her car, Scott raised his eyes to see a black BMW parked across the street. He couldn't make out the driver in the rain. Kathy drove away, then the BMW started up and drove off in the other direction.

It started to rain much harder.

***

Two days later, Scott and Grace attended Frank Johnson's funeral service along with Brittany

Johnson and thirty or forty members of their church. Kathy Becker and several executives from Bell Intelliservices sat, staid and sincere looking, in the tiny sanctuary. Scott didn't claim to be spiritual, but he did respect faith, at least enough to be in church during the important times—Christmas, Easter, and funerals. Long work hours, health issues, and time with Grace left little room in his life for anything else. Maybe now that he wasn't working he could find a little more time for religion.

The minister did his best to comfort Brittany and the others in attendance, but Scott could tell there was very little to say. Frank had been depressed and despondent and couldn't see any other way out. The fact that he and others in attendance that day may have contributed anything to cause Frank's state, or had failed to prevent his death, added a sense of hopelessness to the affair. Stained glass windows throughout the sanctuary encouraged parishioners with images of Jesus healing the sick, Jesus walking on the water and Jesus rising from the tomb. But in truth, everything seemed quite hopeless.

Church, religion in general, was supposed to give hope. People were supposed to come away feeling good, like someone or something was in control and was working to make life better. Without the positive, the facility seemed old and cold, void of meaning. There was no spirit.

The recent hallucination made no sense to Scott. How could he envision such an event with such clarity? The images were so frightening and inexplicable he and Grace had sworn to keep them as solemn secrets. They could never explain them.

After a while, they didn't want to.

Scott struggled to find something, anything he could have said to prevent this tragic and senseless end. He replayed the conversation with Frank. He recalled the hallucination he had that night. He told himself if he had a re-do, he would've acted the same, would have done the same things he had done that day. He couldn't change things, no matter how much he wanted to.

After the service, everyone returned to their cars, to their own lives and to their jobs, if they had them. Talk was brief and solemn.

When he and Grace reached their Prius, Scott unlocked the passenger door and opened it for her. Looking up, he spotted a BMW parked off to the side and beyond most of the other cars in the parking lot. Its black surface glimmered even though the sky was dark. He wondered if the car was the same one parked in front of his house when Kathy Becker visited him. He wondered if she had put him under surveillance or if the Beemer have anything to do with Frank Johnson's death.

"Wait here, just a moment," Scott told Grace and started to walk toward the car.

The driver gunned the engine and sped away before he could get closer.

***

Four days after Bell Intelliservices laid him off, Scott woke up, showered, put on a suit and tie, and drove to the offices of Baker, Grigsby, Landry, and Spicer, the outplacement firm contracted to help those who had been a part of the reorganization. Their offices occupied much of a new multi-floor office building in an office park of similar office buildings. As he drove there, Scott imagined each one housing its own army of outsourcing specialists, laying off hundreds of employees each day, and reassigning them to other offices in other parts of the city. Rearranging furniture on the Titanic.

Organizations like this are a necessary evil. Scott hated them even though he had used their services many times before. They helped some folks find new jobs in tough times. But they also profited on the misfortunes of former employees who were hurting. Most of all, they existed to appease the personal guilt executives felt about causing such layoffs, helping those people feel better about their poor decisions. Besides, Scott knew more about the firing and hiring process than any of the former legal, sales, and operations personnel who had found new careers in outplacement firms.

Scott ducked his head and kept his eyes low as he entered the lobby, which was filled with former employees from Bell Intelliservices. He recognized most of the faces and knew several of the people in the lobby by name. He had always been on the other side of the fence, sentencing countless employees to these offices, but now he was one of the condemned.

The receptionist welcomed him as he signed his name on the register at the front desk. He took a seat in a cloth-bound metal-framed chair next to a young man whom he didn't recognize to await his turn. Sitting with a stranger was easier than trying to explain his situation to employees he had laid off a few days previously. He wanted to blend in.

"My name is Chris Azorin," the man sitting next to him said, extending his hand. He was just a kid—couldn't be more than twenty or twenty-one. His jet black hair curled over his ears and his smile disarmed the most protective. Goatees were a fading fad these days, but Chris sported his like a medal.

"Scott Moore," he said shaking Chris' hand. "Were you from Bell?"

"No, man," Chris said. "You?"

"Me and just about everybody else in this room," Scott said, motioning with his hand.

"Recent layoffs?" Chris asked.

Scott detected a slight, well-hidden Hispanic accent. "Yeah. Four days ago." He looked around the lobby again, recalling the recent changes.

"That's tough. I heard HR over there was pretty ruthless," Chris said.

Scott chuckled under his breath. To his knowledge, "ruthless" was a word that had never been used to describe him.

"So what did you do there?" the talkative young man asked.

"I was the Assistant Director of HR," Scott replied without emotion.

Chris said nothing for a second and then added, "Sorry, but you just don't look that ruthless to me."

Scott chuckled again. "Not all of us are." Then, as an afterthought, added, "Maybe that's why I'm here today. I guess I should have been meaner."

The two sat in silence while others came in and out of the buzzing lobby. One or two former workers nodded to Scott but most thumbed through magazines, or sat, looking nervous and impatient while awaiting the next step.

Scott examined his new acquaintance. Chris was of Hispanic descent. He was wired—cocked and ready to go, leaning forward and tapping his foot or his knee or his fingers. "What brings you here," Scott asked, out of curiosity and in an effort to stop the constant, irritating tapping.

"A program with Tech," he replied. "I just graduated last month. The university works with this firm to help place some of its graduates."

"Some?"

"Yeah. I had a special scholarship. I'll go back to start my doctoral work next term, but the school wants to place us with local companies in a joint work/share program in between terms."

"Like an internship?"

"Yeah. You could call it that. But it's supposed to be more like full employment, with pay and benefits."

"Sounds nice. What did you study?" He was somewhat interested. One day, such knowledge might pay off for Scott were he to implement a similar program in another company.

"Electrical Engineering, with an emphasis on photovoltaic cell design."

Scott felt his eyes grow wide. This kid sounded amazing. "That sounds sophisticated."

"I don't know. They'll probably stick me in some local electric company and I'll be hanging from a telephone pole stringing cable."

"Photovoltaic cell design?"

Chris brushed off his surprised look. "The sun. It always interested me. I grew up in East Texas and sunlight was about all we had." He resumed his tapping.

The two sat in silence for a few more minutes. Their interaction piqued Scott's interest and challenged him to do something for another when he, himself, was struggling. "Look, Chris," he offered. "I may know someone you could contact. He works with Solar Ventures or Soltech or something like that over in Duluth. Give me your contact information and I'll try to arrange a meet up for you."

"Wow, man. That would be great." He dictated his name, cell phone, and email address and Scott jotted them down in his notebook. He didn't know if he could help the kid, but he always took the view that it never hurt to lend a hand when possible.

Then the receptionist called Scott's name and the two exchanged friendly goodbyes.

The rest of the afternoon was an endless litany of things he already knew; things he had been paid to know, things he had taught others in previous roles. Because of his pay grade, he received special one-on-one treatment. They talked about resumes and target companies and career goals. He listed every name of every person he knew and even some that he didn't know, but were friends of friends of his. They gave him a large, handsome, loose-leaf notebook with charts and graphs and exercises, lots of exercises.

He knew the routine as well as his advisor— connect with as many people as possible and use those relationships to connect with more. Find the invisible jobs that weren't posted. Find the ones that weren't even vacant yet, then, be ready with a customized resume and the right elevator pitch to seal the deal. And most important, stay busy. Stay hungry. Keep working on getting work. He now was a full-time job hunter.

Scott wrapped up the session for the day, confirming appointments for later in the week, and headed out the front doors of Baker, Grigsby, Landry, and Spicer. It was a welcome relief to get outside in the fresh air.

Grace was working the late shift again and Scott felt wound up, so he decided to spend an hour or so burning energy at his local gym. No one was exercising, except a handful of guys here or there lifting heavy weights or riding stationary bikes. Despite the air conditioning, the stale scent of sweat emanated from a nearby basket of damp towels. Gary, the night trainer greeted him after signing in.

"Haven't seen you around much lately, Scott."

"Yeah. Been busy."

"Looks like you haven't been eating. You've lost weight."

And he had. Severe stress, as he had just experienced, tended to have that effect. In just a few days his waistline had shrunk and his weight had dropped. He assumed both would increase again in the near future—a stress-induced roller coaster.

After stretching, he climbed aboard an elliptical machine and set an aggressive course, pumping his legs and thrusting his arms.

Forty-five minutes into the routine he felt a pang

of nausea. He punched a few buttons, lowering the intensity level of the machine. Seconds later, the room spun around in a circle and he struggled to hang onto the arms of the apparatus. His knees buckled, banging against the steel foot pedals and he went down, bouncing off the base of the elliptical and sliding to the floor. The fluorescent overhead lights stabbed his eyes. People shouted far away. Some sticky, burning hot liquid slid down the back of his throat and everything went dark.

CHAPTER THREE

Someone said something, but he couldn't make out the words. They became louder, more insistent.

Scott listened and waited for the image to come into focus.

The words weren't in English, but Spanish. He tried to translate but they spoke too fast.

Light came in through a small window on the wall at the back of the house. A man and a woman were chattering as they threw some items—shoes, underwear, and a couple of t-shirts—into an old knapsack. A car horn blared outside.

The sun had gone and he found himself in the back of an old pickup truck, packed with several Hispanics, that rocked and bounced through the night. Dust, thrown up from the dirt road they travelled on, caught in his throat making him cough.

One of the men, the one who had been in the room packing, turned to face him and said, "Esto es emocionante. Vamos a América, donde todos tendremos más oportunidades."

"Hablar en Inglés. Él tiene que acostumbrarse a Inglés," *the woman said.*

The young man nodded and said, "This is exciting. We're going to America where we will all have a better life."

The woman smiled and leaned in through the out-of-focus haze and said, "We are so excited."

In a flash he was older and out of the truck and in the back seat of a car, bare skin of his ass rubbing against vinyl seats. The blonde, who couldn't be more than sixteen years old, rode him like a cowgirl. His hands were up her sweater and under her bra and his fingers squeezed and twisted her nipples. Her squeals became more intense.

The girl leaned forward, blonde hair falling into her face and placed her hands on his bare chest so she could grind herself into him harder. "Ooohhh, shit. Fuck me you Goddamn Dago." She leaned forward farther and kissed him. He tasted strawberry lipstick.

The haze shifted and the girl's nasal cries faded away and he looked into the eyes of a tiny baby, obviously just born, ruddy complexion blending across its face, eyes shut tight, and mouth making small sucking movements.

"She's hungry, honey. Let me have her back."

His hands placed the infant into the woman's arms and he noticed that she was not the same girl he had just been with. She was much older, with jet black hair that clung to her forehead with what must have been dried sweat. His hands reached out to brush her hair away. They were in a hospital somewhere. The woman drew the infant to her breast, which she had pulled from her nightshirt, and it made quiet sucking noises.

The world around him continued to shift, change, blend.

In the background he heard music playing some college theme song. He was standing behind someone dressed in a robe. When he looked down, he noted that he, too, was wearing a robe.

"Hey, man. Are you okay?"

Something pungent rammed through his nostrils and dragged Scott awake. The scent jerked him into an upright sitting position.

"Looks like you passed out," Gary said, tossing away something white and smelly that he had held beneath Scott's nose. He helped Scott crawl to the wall and lean back against it. "Pull your knees up and rest with your head between them," he said.

He knelt beside Scott and checked his pulse and temperature.

"I'm okay," Scott said. "Just give me a moment." A wave of headaches pounded his skull.

"You should go to the ER," Gary said. "Let me call for an ambulance."

"Not necessary. I just slipped, Gary." He shook off the nausea and dizziness and gulped in deep breaths of air.

"You'd better take it easy the rest of the day," Gary suggested.

"Good advice." Scott got up and wobbled to the men's locker room where he showered and dressed.

The seizures were coming more often these days. He wondered what triggered them. Probably stress.

The cool night air took his breath away when he stepped outside into the parking lot. He threw his gear into the back of the Prius and opened the driver's door. Looking up across the top of the car, he spied a black BMW parked at the end of the lot. He started to round the back of his car and inspect the BMW, but his head ached too much. "Fuck it," he said and climbed into the Prius and headed home. At the parking lot exit, he paused and looked again at the black car, wondering if there was any possibility it had anything to do with his hallucinations. "No way," he concluded and drove out of the lot for home.

***

Jeff Gray was an old friend from college. At the last reunion he boasted that he worked at a high-tech startup focusing on green energy. He lived about twenty miles away in Duluth. After fumbling around with online search engines, Scott found a phone number for Solterra, Inc. and made the call. A polite receptionist transferred him to a polite secretary who politely placed him on hold.

"Jeff Gray speaking," the voice said.

"Jeff?" Scott wondered why he always repeated the person's name when he had already said who he was. He also cringed at Jeff's use of the word, "speaking." He wasn't singing. He wasn't shouting. Of course he was speaking.

"Yes."

"Hi, Jeff. This is Scott Moore."

"Oh, hi, Scott. Haven't seen you since the reunion."

"How've you been?"

"As good as I can, considering all the dumb shit they make you do to get government compliance around here. The goddamn regulations are hideous."

"How's your wife?"

"Amy is good, I guess. She stays busy with this group or that. Spends a lot of time at the club, which is where I wish I was right now, on the back nine." He didn't ask about Scott and Grace.

"Say, I ran into a Tech grad the other day—sharp kid. He seemed really personable. Are you guys hiring now?"

"No, not right now. The owner keeps a tight handle on the purse strings."

"That's too bad. This kid graduated high in his class and is returning next term for doctoral work. Said he's studying electrical engineering and specializing in photovoltaic design or something like that." Scott scrutinized his notes to get it right. "Said the grad school would work with the right company to help him get established while he got his degree."

"Sounds like a smart kid," Jeff said. "Probably all head knowledge and no practical experience."

"He may be worth a look," Scott added, drumming his pen on the table. "How about if I buy you both breakfast."

"Well, if you put it that way, I guess I could squeeze in a breakfast meeting."

The two nailed down the specifics for the meeting and ended the conversation. Jeff never asked about Scott's situation.

Scott shrugged it off and keyed in the number Chris had given him. If Chris proved to be a valuable employee, it might lead to something down the road. It never hurt to pay it forward.

"*Hola*," a voice said on the other end. In the background Scott could hear a loud Hispanic television or radio broadcast.

"Hello. Uh, I'd like to speak to Chris Azorin."

"*Que? No habla Inglés.*"

Scott's Spanish sucked. "*Yo hablo Chris Azorin.*"

"*Un momento, por favor.*"

After a moment, "Hello? This is Chris."

"Hi, Chris? This is Scott Moore. We met at the outplacement center a few days ago."

"Oh, yes, Mr. Moore. How are you?"

"I'm doing fine. Yourself?"

"Just getting ready for next term," he said. "My classes look pretty tough."

"How's the employment situation?"

"Nothing, yet. I've talked with some people at several electric companies. You?"

"It'll take time," Scott said. "Say, I remembered the name of a friend of mine who works in a green energy startup over in Duluth. He may be someone you could connect with."

"Oh, wow. That sounds fantastic."

"Yeah. Could you make breakfast on Thursday? I could introduce you two. His name is Jeff Gray and he works with Solterra, Inc. Heard of it?"

"No, I don't think so. But we mostly focused on theory in undergrad."

"Keep that between you and me, okay?" Scott said. Then he added, "I don't know if anything will come of this, but it's a free breakfast. You in?"

"Yeah."

They shared details and ended the call. As he set the phone down, Scott felt positive, proud—better than he'd felt in a long time. Like maybe, he was doing something good.

CHAPTER FOUR

Scott arrived at Jasper's Breakfast House at 8:00 A.M. Jasper's served breakfast and lunch—no dinner—in an upscale atmosphere decked out with beechwood tables and bright colors. They specialized in skillet breakfasts with anything and everything from sausage, ham, steak, bacon, cheese, and all the trimmings over eggs and potatoes. Smells of spices and fried meats and toasting breads mixed with coffee and antiseptic cleaner welcomed guests to the diner.

Chris arrived right on time and pulled up a chair. "Wow. I've never been here," he said, staring around the small restaurant. "This is really nice of you. You don't know me—we hardly met. And yet, you go out of your way to introduce me to...what's his name?"

"Jeff Gray, and he's an operations director at Solterra. It's a good little startup with a lot of potential."

"Well, thanks for helping me out."

"No problem. It's what I do," Scott said. "Did

you bring your resume?"

"Yeah." He handed over a couple of pages stapled together.

Chris perused the document. He had seen thousands in his day, and he knew exactly where to look and exactly which red flags to look for. "Says you were born in San Antonio, right?"

"Uh, yes, sir. Of course, I don't remember that…"

Scott chuckled at Chris' effort to be funny, assuming the kid was nervous. "Might not want to mention that to Jeff. It may not come across as funny to him."

"Yes, sir."

"Then again, it could be that I've heard it before."

"Oh. I also brought my transcripts," Chris said, handing an official looking copy to him. He tapped the table with his fingers as if he was pounding a drum.

"These are impressive grades," Chris said. "Can you keep that up in graduate school?"

"I think so. College wasn't that tough."

"Very good," Scott said. "Let's hope Jeff is just as impressed. Let me warn you, he'll do whatever he can to make your stuff seem normal or average. I don't know why he does it. Maybe it's a defense mechanism or something, but he talks down everything and everybody."

"Okay," Chris said.

"Here he is."

Jeff wore middle age like a kid who had to wear his dad's tie to a middle school dance—reluctantly.

His receding hairline had taken over most of his round melon and his belly hung over his belt like an extra layer of clothes. He was a heart attack that had waited to happen five years too long.

"Hey, Jeff," Scott stood and welcomed his old friend with a handshake. Then he added, "You've shaved your beard!"

"Yeah. The wife insisted I take it off," he said. "Said it scratched her when we did the dirty." He grinned as only Jeff could.

Scott frowned.

"This all looks good. I'll have one skillet with everything in it and an extra side of biscuits," he said as he plopped down in the empty chair. "I tell you, Amy has me on this bran diet and I'm shitting wheat fields. And gas—don't sit too close boys—it'll make your eyes water."

"Sounds rough," Scott said. "Meet Chris Azorin."

"Yeah. Nice to meet you," Jeff nodded in his direction. "Can we order?"

They feasted on fried, scrambled, and poached eggs topped with virtually every topping known to man. Jeff went on a protein and carb binge and came up only after he had wiped the skillet clean with his last biscuit. Jeff and Scott put away three pots of black coffee and Chris drank lots of water, finishing it off with a tall glass of orange juice.

"I've seen better," Jeff said, glancing over Chris' resume and turning his attention to his transcripts. "Not bad, but we've already got some pretty sharp cookies in our company."

Chris looked like he had been hit by a truck.

"Look, we don't have anything right now, but something may open up. Mind if I keep these?"

"Sure," Chris said. "I can provide more information, maybe references?"

"I'll call you if I want 'em." He backed away from the table. "I gotta run, boys. Got a staff meeting at ten."

They all shook hands, and Jeff hustled out the front door after asking the waitress for a large cup of coffee to go.

Chris looked beaten.

"I warned you not to worry about Jeff," Scott said. "He grows on you over time."

"Really?" Chris asked.

"No. That's the way he always is. But he liked what he saw."

"How can you tell?"

"'Cause I'm a people person."

They chatted for thirty more minutes and then stood to go their separate ways. Scott paid for breakfast and left a generous tip.

"You really think I've got a chance, Mr. Moore?" Chris asked in the parking lot.

"Count on it, Chris."

Chris climbed into a red Honda Civic sporting Tech bumper stickers and sped away. Two cars were left in the parking lot this late in the morning—Scott's Prius and a black BMW.

He marched directly across the lot towards the luxury vehicle. To his surprise, it didn't drive away, but remained stationary. As he neared, the smoky driver's window lowered, revealing a lone figure sitting behind the wheel. "Hello, Mr. Moore. I'm

Dr. Paul Blackwell." The man extended his hand through the window.

Scott shook his hand carefully. "You've been following me."

"Research," the man said. A knowing and somewhat vile smile visible beneath a gray goatee.

"What do you want?"

"Let's go inside and chat, shall we?"

***

Paul Blackwell exuded professor—but the worst professor on campus. His dark, but fast-graying hair was slicked back as if trying to escape his bulbous forehead. The mustache began inside his nostrils as nose hair and flowed down over the upper lip ending just shy of his teeth. The bottom portion of the goatee gave him an evil, devil look. Wire rim glasses, fashionable in an earlier time and place, threatened to slide down his sweaty nose.

The two men ordered cups of coffee, the fourth cup for Scott, and examined each other for a moment.

"I haven't been following you, Scott, but I have been watching."

"What's the difference?"

"I think it's a matter of motive." He unfolded the napkin and shook it once before draping it in his lap. "A follower, a stalker if you will, follows for what he can get from the individual—personal gratification or some strange semi-erotic pleasure."

"And why have you followed me?"

"Watched you, my friend," Dr. Blackwell

49

interrupted. "Someone who watches does so because he can help the other."

"You're splitting hairs." He sipped the bitter coffee and felt himself wince.

"Perhaps, but maybe not. A neighbor watches your backyard and warns you if your hot tub overflows, or if your dog runs off, or if a limb has broken on a tree in your backyard and is threatening to fall on your roof."

His detailed descriptions, straight out of his own yard, chilled Scott's bones. He scrutinized the man's features. "You said you could help me. How?"

His single-word question opened the door to further inquiry and the doctor slipped through. "You've fallen on some tough times lately, haven't you?"

"I've been through tougher."

"Do the visions increase in times of stress?"

His words surprised Scott. To date only Grace and a couple of physicians were aware that he experienced hallucinations. They attributed them to early-onset Alzheimer's or transient ischemic attacks—TIAs, once described to him as tiny strokes. Scott proceeded with caution. "I tend to have hallucinations more often when I'm stressed," he said. "How did you know?"

"Oh, Scott. I know a great deal about you."

Dr. Blackwell waited. The question remained on the table.

The waitress came and filled their coffee cups and the two men sipped in silence.

Scott waited.

Dr. Blackwell said, "I received my doctorate in Paranormal Psychology from Emory University. In that program, I made some amazing discoveries. Some of my research took me to Latvia, in particular to Riga, a port city on the Baltic Sea. Have you heard of it?"

"No, I don't recall that I have."

"You were born there, Scott."

"That's where your research is wrong," Scott said. "I was born in Orlando, Florida."

"Either you've been misinformed or you are not being honest with me. You grew up in Orlando, Florida, but your parents, Ron and Cheryl Moore adopted you as an infant. Am I right?"

Right as rain. Scott's parents told him his birth mother lived in Orlando. He had never questioned their word, so he had no proof either way.

"Allow me to back up a bit, all right?" Dr. Blackwell asked. "Your birth mother was Evgenia Voznaja. She grew up in Riga, Latvia under the rule of the Soviet Union."

"That's preposterous."

"It's not that unusual. Believe it or don't," he said with a shrug. "It's your prerogative. My doctoral research introduced me to Dr. Konstantins Dekhtyar, a noted psychic researcher from Russia, renowned for his work on 'Remote Viewing', the ability to 'see' events happening at a distance or in a hidden location using paranormal abilities. At the height of the Cold War, Dekhtyar tested the effects of various psychotropic drugs, therapies, and treatments on psychic abilities. The Soviets were attempting to use paranormal abilities to spy on the

Pentagon. Dr. Dekhtyar treated patients with a genetic predisposition to psychic ability with medicines that would heighten their abilities."

Scott interrupted Dr. Blackwell's narrative, "What kind of medicines."

"Unfortunately, most of those records were lost in a fire shortly after he died. I did hear that he tried LSD, but everyone tried LSD back then."

"Was he successful?"

"One of his paid subjects was Mrs. Voznaja, a young, married woman in her twenties who needed the small amount of pay Dr. Dekhtyar offered for the tests. As it turned out she was one of his most promising subjects, in more ways than one."

The story sounded like a bad paperback.

"They became romantically involved and she became pregnant. The husband was sterile so he figured out she had been unfaithful. Dekhtyar successfully hid her from her husband until after the infant—you—were born. He used his influence to have you sent to the states and adopted in Florida. That was 1973, the year you were born."

"And where is my birth mother now?"

"Her jealous husband shot her and Dr. Dekhtyar, and turned the gun on himself just days after you arrived in the U.S. It set the Soviet's psychic research program back several years. It never recovered."

"That's a pretty wild story, Doc. So you've been following me around to tell me the real name of my birth mother, right?"

"There's one important detail that you should remember."

"Which is?"

"Your mother underwent much of Dr. Dekhtyar's treatments after you were conceived. The drugs she took also entered your bloodstream while you were a fetus."

"So you're implying that my hallucinations are the result of some psychotropic drugs my mother took before I was born? Over forty years ago?"

"That plus your genetic proclivity for psychic ability. But more than that, I'm suggesting that your visions are actual events. They are not hallucinations."

Someone dropped something in the kitchen and the clash of porcelain on tile resonated through the restaurant.

"I didn't see that coming," Scott said.

"It doesn't work that way," Blackwell answered. "Last week, just after you parted ways with Bell Intelliservices, you experienced an episode—Tuesday, am I correct?"

"How'd you know about that?"

He ignored the question. "What visions did you have during that episode? Do you remember them?"

"They were all jumbled together. They always are."

He accented each word. "What do you remember?"

Scott took a short breath, feeling like a schoolboy asked to recite a poem. "A strange house…at night. It was out of focus."

"Yes," Blackwell said. "Go on."

"I sat down in a recliner—plaid, cloth."

"Ahh. The visions are multi-sensory." The

doctor typed notes on a tablet. Scott hadn't seen him take it out of his briefcase.

As Scott recalled the images, he focused away from the little diner and out the large glass window beside their table. "It seemed like I was in Frank Jackson's house. He worked at Bell. He also killed himself." He turned his gaze back to the doctor.

Dr. Blackwell stopped typing.

"And that was it."

"Do you remember where you were when you had that vision?" He still didn't call it a hallucination. All of the other doctors had.

"You tell me," Scott said. Perhaps this guy was just a clever charlatan. "You're the one who claimed I had an attack on Tuesday."

Dr. Blackwell squinted his eyes and studied Scott's face. "You were on your back porch after being laid off. You soaked in a hot tub."

Scott stared back. He was correct. He had the hallucination in the Jacuzzi. But he had left out the fact that Scott had been drinking.

"Oh, and I believe you were drinking Scotch whisky."

That startled Scott. "You said you wanted to help me. How?"

"Mr. Moore," Dr. Blackwell began. "I believe you and I can work together to manage and possibly help you profit from your gift."

"No way. I'm nobody's guinea pig and I'm not a sideshow freak." He started to collect his belongings to leave.

"Of course not. But you would like to be in more control, wouldn't you? You'd like to keep from having such hallucinations, wouldn't you?" It was the first time he used that word.

"Yes."

"I believe I can be of assistance to you."

"And if I agree?"

"I will pay you for your efforts. In fact, I'm willing to pay twenty-five percent more per month than you received at Bell Intelliservices. If you're ever uncomfortable, just say so, and we will cease our arrangement."

"Let me talk with Grace."

***

"Hell, no! I won't let some quack pump you full of LSD or PCP or any other drug." She was banging pans around in the kitchen. She always banged pans when she was upset. Scott could tell how upset by the volume of the pan banging.

"I work with druggies every night, and I don't want my husband to be one of them."

"He's not going to do that," Scott said. "Besides, he may be able to help me. No one else has."

"He may kill you," she added.

He threw his hand down in disgust. "He's not going to kill me."

She stopped what she was doing. "You don't know anything about him."

"He seems legit." Saying, "legit" made it sound like it had more credibility.

"I want to see a diploma. I want to talk with him. I want references."

When she started making demands, Scott knew

she was weakening. After all, if he could provide those things, could she still resist? "Grace," he said. "I don't think paranormal psychologists have references."

"That's just the point. He sounds like a quack."

Scott wasn't surprised by her hesitation, but something made him feel she wasn't telling everything. "I don't think he's a quack."

"You met him once…at Jasper's Breakfast House."

"Honey, he's also willing to pay me. Let's face it. If I don't land another job in a few months, we may need every cent we can get to make ends meet."

"I'd rather be in the poor house than lose you." It sounded reassuring, but almost too reassuring, perhaps even overplayed.

He walked into the kitchen and put his arms around her, in a constraining way. Struggle as she might, she could not break free. It sent the message that she wouldn't break him of his plans to work with Dr. Blackwell. "Let's just have dinner together. The three of us. We'll take it one step at a time."

"And if he slips us LSD?"

"We'll have a hell of a dinner."

***

They met at a locally owned steakhouse. The steaks were grilled over wood with an unusual marinade, filling the entire restaurant with a smoky oak scent. Thick baked potatoes and a large family-size bowl of mixed vegetables rounded out the meal. For desert, they all chose the house's special cheesecake topped with fruit.

As he knifed the large slice of desert, Dr. Blackwell made his pitch. "I believe we will be able to discover things that no one, to date, has known about man's ultimate abilities. We can open the door to new ways of thinking about communication, creativity, relating and more. We can turn the world on its ear and Scott can make that happen," he said. He seemed to be talking to Grace alone.

"How do we know it will be safe?" Grace interrupted. Scott knew she had been waiting to broach that subject all night. When Dr. Blackwell opened the door, she ran through it.

"We will take every precaution we can. I'll require tests and scans, constant monitoring, whatever is necessary to keep Scott safe. After all, everything depends on his ability and willingness to be tested. It's not like I have people standing in line who were part of Dr. Dekhtyar's original study."

"So you've never tested Dr. Dek, Dek…"

"Dr. Dekhtyar," Dr. Blackwell said.

"You've never tested his hypothesis on anyone else?"

"Oh, back at Emory we ran some students through various exercises. It was all quite benign, and pointless, for that matter. And of course, none of them had received Dekhtyar's original treatment."

"This had better be benign, as well," she said.

"Grace. I promise to keep you informed every step of the way."

"Where will your research take place?"

"I've rented some space in an office complex on Maple. I've hired an assistant and will record and document everything."

"That all sounds expensive. How can you afford this?"

"I consider it to be an investment," Dr. Blackwell said, dabbing up the last crumbs on his plate with his fork. "Besides, I inherited a bit of money from my father who had invested in a good deal of land in the northeast. It won't last forever, but will help us get a good start."

"And we will have the power to stop this if we ever feel it isn't safe?"

"I guarantee it."

Scott listened to the banter in silence. He knew Grace as well as anyone could and felt, for Dr. Blackwell's sake, that it would be best if she never felt it was not safe.

CHAPTER FIVE

Scott's first session with Dr. Blackwell took place four days later. The two men met in his office and shared cups of decaf coffee. The doctor set a rule in the first meeting that they would only drink decaf, if anything, during their meetings.

They worked through a battery of tests and profiles. By the end of the morning, Scott's head throbbed with a powerful headache. That afternoon they drove to a nearby clinic and Scott underwent CT and MRI scans. Technicians drew blood samples and he took a full stress test. They ended back at Dr. Blackwell's office.

"Scott, you've had a couple of episodes in the last two weeks, is that correct?"

"Yes, two."

Scott felt like he was undergoing a lie detector test. "On the day you were laid off, you had a vision and you were under the influence of alcohol at that time."

"Plus, I was relaxing in our hot tub."

"Ahhh, yes. Good point."

"And in the second episode, you were at the gym, having just completed a vigorous workout."

"That's right. I passed out."

"My observation is that the first incident, to some extent, was influenced by a depressant. Alcohol is clearly a depressant. I'm also assuming your workout was tough enough to exhaust you and bring you to a somewhat depressed state."

"That makes sense, I guess."

"So I'd like to begin with some mild sedatives and see if we can duplicate the state you were in during those episodes. If we achieve success, we can adjust the dose to determine if we can learn to manage them."

They shook hands and went separate ways.

Scott couldn't ignore the feeling that he wasn't hearing the complete story.

***

Scott threw the Frisbee and Gumby dashed across the backyard to catch it before it landed. The playful mutt, eyes wide with delight, brought it back to his master. Scott chucked it again as hard as he could as Grace stepped outside carrying a couple of glasses of ice tea. Gumby reached him before she did, so he took the disc dripping with slick saliva, and hurled it toward the neighbor's fence one more time. The frisky boxer lunged off in that direction, eager to retrieve it and go again. By the time he returned, Grace was handing Scott his glass of tea. The dog persisted, though, and pressed the toy to Scott's leg, again and again.

"I just got a phone call from Amy Gray," she said. "We've been invited to their house Sunday afternoon for a cookout."

The news surprised Scott. Jeff Gray was not an outgoing sociable soul. He had never invited Scott and Grace to a cookout before. In fact, the big lumbering executive, intent on money and power, never showed interest in anyone who couldn't provide something in return. Obviously Scott, a former lower level human resources manager, had little to offer Jeff. Until now. He took the Frisbee with his free hand and slung it across the yard. Dog slobber flung off in all directions from the plastic toy. Gumby raced after the Frisbee like a hound chasing a fox.

"They're throwing a party for Jeff's department at Solterra," Grace said. "We haven't seen them both since the reunion a couple of years ago. Sounds fun."

The dog returned again with the damn Frisbee.

"She said Jeff wanted to introduce a new kid he'd hired to his staff at the party. Obviously, spouses are invited."

"Oh, yeah, I met that kid in the outplacement center and introduced him to Jeff," Scott said. "So, I guess he hired the guy." He took the Frisbee from Gumby and tossed it again.

"According to Amy, Jeff is pretty excited."

"How about that," Scott said. "I did something right for a change."

He waited for a reassuring response from Grace denying that he never did anything right, but none came.

61

***

The smell of hot dogs and hamburgers floated out into the street and greeted Scott as soon as he opened his car door. The Grays lived in a white two-story house at the end of a cul-de-sac lined with way-above-average homes. Scott could hear country music playing in the back yard.

Grace, wearing a revealing sundress and sandals, carried a homemade casserole. They approached the front door where Amy greeted them. She was drop-dead gorgeous with long blonde hair and a smile that could stop a truck. Scott never understood what she saw in Jeff. She welcomed them both with a light hug and a peck on the cheek, took the casserole from Grace, and ushered them through the spacious house and to the back yard where the party was in full swing.

Neither he nor Grace knew many of the people gathered around the back yard. Jeff was busy keeping a smoky grill from turning into a five-alarm fire. Other adults sat in chairs scattered here and there, drinking beer or glasses of what looked like ice tea. A few of the younger guys threw a football back and forth while they flexed for the younger women in the department.

"Welcome to my castle," Jeff shouted over his shoulder. "It's not much, but it'll do."

Scott wondered what Jeff thought would be "much." He and Grace lived well, shared a house with two more bedrooms than they used and had never tried the bathroom in the guest room, yet their home did not compare to Jeff's house. A spacious back yard that could have doubled as a golf course green spread out before them. Near the built-in grill, a pond-less water feature gurgled with the sound of a soothing creek.

Jeff called everyone to lunch and Scott and Grace joined the line to pluck some food from the bounty. Scott added a burned chunk of ground cow to a bun, realizing even he had never insulted a hamburger as much as Jeff had this one. After sitting at a picnic table beneath a giant oak, he drowned the patty in steak sauce, pickles, onions, and cheese and hoped for the best. When he bit into the charred mess, steak sauce, onions, pickles, and cheese dripped out of the corners of his mouth.

Chris Azorin delivered his plate full of hot dogs, a hamburger, and mounds of potato chips to the place next to him.

"Mr. Moore," Chris said, extending his hand.

"Chris!" Scott said, first wiping his hand on a napkin and then shaking Chris' vigorously. Then he turned to his wife. "Grace. This is Chris Azorin, the young man I told you about."

Grace nodded from across the table. Chris followed by reaching his hand out and Grace offered hers in response. They seemed to shake hands a moment longer than necessary.

"And, I guess you're also the man of honor at this social event, right Chris?" Grace asked.

"I wouldn't say that," he suggested. "It's just a chance for us all to get to know each other." He didn't take his eyes off Grace.

"You're too humble, young man," Scott answered, placing an arm around his shoulders and turning his body, and focus, away. "I hear they are very pleased to have you at Solterra."

"It is a wonderful place to work. And it wouldn't have happened without your help. I am forever grateful."

"I'm glad it worked out."

Grace turned her attention to a lady next to her who was massaging a burp from a tiny infant resting on her shoulder. The infant seemed to stretch this way and that in a spastic manner, as though he couldn't get comfortable. "Man, there are more good lookin' women in this company than on the entire Tech campus," Chris semi-whispered to Scott. "It is incredible."

"One of the perks, I guess."

"Perks? Oh, Lord," Jeff interrupted as he walked by trying to pass out second helpings of incinerated hamburgers. "Don't get an HR guy talking about perks. We'll be doomed to bankruptcy." He wore a grill apron sporting the words, **'Around here I'm the boss.'**

"I'm just chatting," Scott said.

"How's the burgers?" Jeff asked everyone at the table.

"Delicious! Wonderful! Tasty," everyone lied.

He moved on to another table.

"Talking about delicious, wonderful, and tasty," Chris whispered to Scott.

Scott leaned back and followed the young man's gaze. To his surprise, Amy Gray filled his line of sight. "Whoa, stud," he cautioned. "She's way out of bounds."

"Still, she looks nice," Chris said.

He was right. She may have been the most attractive woman at the event, even counting Grace who, like himself, had gained a little unsightly weight in unwanted areas and a wrinkle or two over the years. He allowed himself to observe Amy from afar. No one would believe that she and Grace were the same age. Her inviting cleavage drew his look past her flat-as-a-pancake stomach to the hips of a twenty-year old. When she turned to speak with a man standing beside her, he could not take his eyes off her perfect ass. When she turned back around, her intoxicating smile caught him off-guard, making him blush and look away.

Instead, he looked into the eyes of his wife, Grace. Busted.

"Having a good time?" she asked.

He felt his face warm up even more.

"Don't encourage him," she mouthed softly.

Chris didn't hear her, but Scott had learned to read her lips and her facial expressions years ago.

Dessert was strawberry shortcake, with fresh strawberries and abundant mounds of whipped cream. Scott rose from the table to get a plate for himself and to fetch another to offer as absolution to his wife. They shared their shortcake apart from the other diners near the stairs leading up to the expansive deck jutting out from Jeff's house.

"You're causing problems," Grace said.

"Huh?" He looked up to catch Chris, hands in pockets and swaying back and forth in an awe-gee fashion as he talked with Amy Gray. She giggled and patted him lightly on his shoulder.

"What are you two talking about?" Jeff asked as

he approached with his own plate piled high with strawberries and whipped cream.

"Oh, nothing," Scott said. "You've got some nice people in your company."

"Don't believe it for a second," Jeff said, washing down his words with a swig of beer. "Most of 'em are lazy freeloaders and all of 'em would stab you in the back if they could."

"Now, Jeff. They're not that bad."

"I have to ride them like a cowboy riding herd," he said. "Otherwise, we wouldn't get anything done."

"Well, they've been nice to us today," Scott said.

"And the food has been delicious," Grace added.

"This new kid is a breath of fresh air," Jeff went on, ignoring the compliments. "I don't want the rest of them to be a bad influence on him. Where'd he go?"

"He's right over there talking with your..." When he looked up, Chris was gone. So was Amy. "I don't know where he went."

"I'm gonna have to put an ankle bracelet on him to keep track," Jeff slurred. "He may try to sneak back across the border."

"What? He's not undocumented, is he?"

"Hell if I know. That's HR's problem. And you know HR never makes mistakes," he quipped.

Scott ignored the dig, but tucked the thought away in the back of his mind.

CHAPTER SIX

"Come in, Scott," Dr. Blackwell said while he pounded on his keyboard. "Let me make just a few more notes and then we can get started. By the way, did you take a cab this morning as we discussed?"

"Yes, sir."

"Just leave a receipt and I'll reimburse you. We're going to try a little medication today and I don't think it would be wise to drive."

"Whatever." He pulled up the padded arm chair. It was much nicer than the office chair he used back in Bell. In fact, all of the office trappings were nicer. An ornate clock sat atop a walnut bookcase which matched picture frames strategically placed along the walls. What was absent were pictures of anyone but Dr. Blackwell. It gave him the feeling he was being watched from various locations around the office. Several had adorned Scott's desk—photos of Grace, he and Grace and even Gumby reminding him of the important things in his life. He wondered what the important things were in Dr. Blackwell's life.

"Now, how are you today," Dr. Blackwell asked, peering over the top of his glasses. The two men went through the daily routine of checking in and comparing notes. "Now, Scott, I want to try a light dose of Alprazolam. It's a mild sedative, often used to help people with anxiety disorders or panic attacks."

"But I'm not anxious."

"Of course not," the doctor responded. "However, it is my belief that the Alprazolam, Xanax is the trade name, will work to relax you and allow you be more receptive to the visions that you have. Worse case, you'll feel very relaxed and go home to a nice nap. It's a very common medication that is used all over the world with very few side effects."

"What are those side effects?"

He dismissed his concern with a wave of his hand. "Drowsiness, dizziness, maybe a skin rash. But in the small dosage I'm administering, you don't have anything to worry about."

Scott rolled up his sleeve as the doctor filled a syringe with liquid from a small medicine bottle. He tensed his muscles just before feeling a stab from the sharp needle.

As Dr. Blackwell administered the drug, he said, "Just relax and allow your mind to wander."

Scott leaned back in his armchair and felt the medication take effect. He began to feel comfortable and then...content.

Dr. Blackwell tapped out some notes on is laptop. After several minutes, he turned back to Scott. "How do you feel?"

"I'm fine. How are you?"

"The sedative is taking effect?" Dr. Blackwell asked Scott.

"Yes, it is."

The doctor looked up from his glass-covered desk and called out to the receptionist in the other room. "Debbie. Are you ready?"

"I'll be right in," the thin brunette called back.

Scott had seen Debbie every day for the last week, but had not taken time to say more than hello to her. He stood, reached out a hand which she took in hers. "Hi," Scott said. She returned the greeting.

Debbie carried a notebook and pen and sat in the other arm chair. A strong whiff of peppermint drifted from her smacking lips.

"You won't need the pad," Dr. Blackwell instructed.

She set the pad and pen on the floor beside her chair.

"What should I do?" Debbie asked.

"Just sit still for a while."

"Sure. Whatever." She chewed her gum more quickly.

"Um, would you mind?" The doctor asked, pointing to his own cheek.

"Oh, not at all," she answered, looking about nervously before tearing off a piece of paper and depositing the gum onto it. She wrapped that up and set it on top of the steno pad.

"Now, Scott, reach across and take Ms. Taylor's hand. I want you to focus on relaxing. Ignore all distractions. Concentrate only on Ms. Taylor."

Scott obediently took the receptionist's hand in

his own and willfully forced his mind to focus on the receptionist. He stared at her like a physician might scrutinize a patient, which only made his head hurt.

"Close your eyes. Let go. Let it happen. Allow your mind to focus on Ms. Taylor."

He obeyed, but felt nothing.

"Scott," Dr. Blackwell interrupted.

Opening his eyes, Scott looked to the doctor.

"Listen to Ms. Taylor…with your mind and your heart."

Returning his attention to Debbie, Scott closed his eyes and began to sink into a state of semi-consciousness.

He heard voices. Someone was talking. Children were pointing. Laughing. He was on a school playground, covered with snow.

"Tell me what you see."

"I'm…I'm at a school—the playground. There are children pointing at me and laughing." Scott began to shiver. "I'm cold. I'm not wearing a coat."

"Is it winter?"

"Yes, I think so. The sky is gray, like it gets just before a snowfall. My new coat is on the ground. Some children are stomping on it."

"Excellent. Can you see anything else?"

Scott felt Debbie's hand tighten. "They've also taken my lunchbox. They're laughing at what my mother packed. Someone said they thought I brought two lunch boxes each day because I was so fat."

"Yes. Go on."

Her hand dripped with sweat. "They are calling me names. Fatty, Piggy. More children are coming and a crowd is gathering. Someone else is coming. I think it's a teacher."

"No," Debbie said, snatching her hand away. "It's the school principal."

Her voice and actions pulled Scott back into a semiconscious state.

"Do you remember this event?" Scott heard Dr. Blackwell ask.

"Yes," Debbie replied.

"Okay, Scott. Let this episode go."

Scott did as he was told. The images faded with the sounds. He looked around the office, feeling as if he'd just broken the surface after swimming underwater. He noticed Debbie was clenching her hands together in her lap.

"So the event actually happened?" Dr. Blackwell spoke to Debbie.

Her hands were shaking and her voice followed suit. "Yes. It happened when I was nine or ten years old," she replied. "The boys called me names. They pushed me around the playground and pulled off my coat."

"Were there teachers around?"

"No. The teachers were inside." Her voice trembled.

"What happened then?"

"They called me names, as he said. I was a bit overweight at the time. They said I was fat."

"Do you consider that to be a major event in your life?" Dr. Blackwell asked.

"No shit. I hated myself. I stopped eating. I taught myself to stick my finger down my throat after meals to throw up."

Scott stared at the thin lady. He understood her. He sensed she struggled with bulimia and it somehow made sense. He felt a surge of embarrassment.

"Months of therapy and behavior modification eventually taught me to like myself again," she said. "It took a long time." She turned to Scott. "Your retelling of that event brought back one of the most painful times of my life." Tears welled up in her eyes and began to roll down her face, mussing her makeup. Pain burned in her eyes.

"I'm sorry," Scott said. "I didn't know…"

"No," Dr. Blackwell interrupted. "That was perfect. You were able to view a complete event in another person's life. Tell me. How did the images appear? Were the sounds clear?" He leaned forward on his elbows, lapping up the information like a hungry dog eating dinner.

"It was much more vivid than my hallucinations—much clearer," Scott said. "It was as if I was experiencing a story—someone else's story—while it played out. It was realistic, as if I was there, but as if I shouldn't have been there at the same time."

"And you were in control, right?"

"That's correct. When you told me to stop, I was able to stop."

Debbie was wiping her eyes with a tissue.

"Are you okay?" Scott asked.

"Yes," she said. "It hurt. I haven't thought about

that in a long time."

"But accurate, right?"

"Yes," she said softly. "On target." She rose from the chair slowly and returned to the front office, leaving her stenographer's pad and pen, as well as the wadded-up chewing gum, behind.

"I must collect my notes," Dr. Blackwell said, turning his chair and typing details into his computer. "Please relax for a bit, Scott. I will call a cab for you in a few moments. You must rest the remainder of the day."

Scott did as he was told. In a few moments, the cab arrived and he stood up, preparing to return home. "Bye, Dr. Blackwell," he said.

"Tomorrow. I'll see you tomorrow at the same time." He never looked up from the computer monitor.

When Scott walked by the receptionist's desk, Debbie was no longer there.

***

Dr. Blackwell had insisted that Scott take a cab to the office the next day, as well. "At least until we have the correct dosage of alprazolam," he'd added. When Scott arrived at the doctor's office, he noticed Debbie wasn't at her desk. Instead, an older lady occupied her seat. She was not chewing gum.

"Hi," he said. "I'm Scott Moore. I have an appointment with Dr. Blackwell."

"He's expecting you," she said cheerily. "Go right on in."

He knocked on the doorjamb and called out,

"Hello? Dr. Blackwell?"

"Yes, Scott," Dr. Blackwell said wiping his hands on a towel as he stepped from a restroom in the corner of his office.

They shook hands.

The doctor turned to his desk, pumped some hand sanitizer onto his palms, and rubbed them together. "How was the night?" Dr. Blackwell asked.

"Very good. I can't remember when I've slept so soundly," Scott answered.

"I am so excited about our progress. I believe we made some great advances yesterday."

"I noticed Debbie wasn't at her desk. Is she all right?"

"I'm sure she will be fine. She decided this job wasn't what she was looking for."

"Did she leave because of yesterday's incident?" Scott asked. "It felt kinda creepy."

"It doesn't really matter why she left."

"It does to me," Scott argued. "Recalling the story seemed to hurt her."

"Her memory of something that happened long ago hurt her," Blackwell countered.

"Do we have the right to dredge up such painful memories?" Scott stared at Dr. Blackwell, sensing they had reached an impasse.

"She was well compensated for her pain," Blackwell said. "Did you meet our new receptionist, Elizabeth?"

"I said hi," Scott said.

"Are you ready to start?"

"Let's do it."

"Today, I've invited two gentlemen to join us. I would like to apply a slightly higher dose of Alprazolam—we'll use a pill this time—and I'd like you to read each of them."

"Are they here?"

"They should arrive in a few moments," he said. "I'd also like to try this experiment 'blind', if you will. I won't tell them what we're about."

"But won't they feel weird when we hold hands?"

The doctor chuckled. "I want you to simply shake hands with them when they enter the room. Some research indicates a simple touch may trigger psychometry."

"What?"

"The ability to see experiences—stories as you call them, that other people have," Dr. Blackwell said in a professorial tone. Scott half-expected there would be a final exam.

"It's your show." He accepted a small white pill and a glass of water and started to ease back down in the arm chair. He welcomed the relaxing effect of the medication as one might welcome a familiar song or a gratifying phone call. He closed his eyes, but could hear the doctor moving around behind him, greeting the others as they entered the office.

After a moment, the doctor said, "Scott. I have two gentlemen here in the office with us."

Scott stood to greet the two men. One was middle-aged, with rugged features and short, almost crew-cut short, hair. The other was thin and pasty and quite a bit older than the first. They shook hands and exchanged greetings.

"Follow the same procedure as yesterday and tell me what you can," Dr. Blackwell said.

He sat back in the chair, closed his eyes and relaxed and allowed himself to "listen" with his heart and his mind. Their stories appeared even more clear than Debbie's. "This is interesting," he said. "I see a dark area, like a theater, but without seats. Two or three images are suspended before me, like choices or selections. Like a menu. I'm going to choose the one on the left."

"Continue," Dr. Blackwell said.

Scott heard soft music playing in the background. It sounded like an old AM radio. He blinked his eyes several times to counter the effect of bright lights overhead.

He was in a store—a hardware store. Most of the racks and shelves seemed new. A display announced, "Now! A Cordless Power Drill" in bright letters.

"I'm in a hardware store. There's a polished vinyl floor and the shelves all look new. There are a few balloons and a small crowd of shoppers."

"Go ahead," the doctor said.

"Now, I'm holding a dollar bill and shaking someone's hand. I set the dollar bill in the bottom of the register, which, by the way, is not computerized—it's one of the old style registers."

He left that scene to view another and stood before a casket in what appeared to be a funeral home. "I hear organ music. I'm at a funeral," he announced. "There's a young woman with black

76

hair and glasses in the coffin. I'm gripping the side. Now someone is escorting me to my seat. Everything's blurry—I'm crying."

He heard someone in the room clear his throat.

"Now, I'm going to focus on the other gentleman," Scott said.

"Very well," Dr. Blackwell said.

"There are several images to choose from. Scott could hear the click-clack of typing. He thought it came from the doctor's desk, but he couldn't be sure.

The typing sound faded and was replaced by another. "I hear alarms, a loud bell, and sirens. Shouting. I'm in an older neighborhood, moving fast. There's a fire. Hot. I'm running inside the house, upstairs. More shouting. I'm in a bedroom, a child's bedroom. It's smoky, but I don't smell the smoke. I'm wearing an oxygen mask—some kind of breathing apparatus. Someone's hiding in the corner, coughing. He's calling for help."

He returned to the dark room and moved toward another image.

Scott saw himself gather up a child in a blanket and turn to run down burning stairs and out the front door. Someone took the child from him and he stumbled to a fire truck to catch his breath.

"Now I'm seeing something else. It's windy. I'm standing on a ledge, high up—a mountain. I see a huge canyon, like the Grand Canyon. The sun is playing off the ridges in the distance. It's...inspiring."

He was back in the black room, again. He chose another of the images and approached it.

Loud country and western music surrounded him.

"I'm talking with an attractive redhead in a bar, a country-western bar. She has a pretty smile. It's crowded." Within moments, he felt himself moving back and forth to the music, yet he knew he still sat in the chair.

"The location has changed. It's quieter. The same woman is here, but we're in someone's home. I feel like it's not familiar." He made a conscious effort to back out of that scene and into another.

"I'm seeing something else, now. It's another fire. Loud noises—alarms, bells."

He was in a house, no, a larger building. It was a church.

"I'm in a sanctuary. Pews, red carpet. It isn't a large church. It's hot. I feel like I'm choking—can't get enough oxygen. The fire is above me, around me. Chunks of the ceiling are falling all around. I'm scared."

He entered the last scene window and everything was quiet. "I hear music in the background, but it's very faint. Wow. I smell a strong odor—urine, antiseptic."

He looked out over the same canyon he had seen earlier.

"I'm at the canyon again. I'm holding up my hands and my skin seems dried out and wrinkled. I've got blemishes, scars, moles. My fingernails are yellow."

The canyon began to move away.

"Wait. I'm not outside. The canyon is a photograph in a picture frame. Looking around the room, I see it is fairly empty. A window is against one wall. Very little furniture. A lamp on a small bedside table. The picture frame sits beneath the lamp."

"Okay, Scott," Dr. Blackwell's voice said. "Come on back now."

Scott felt himself move out of the dream-state, past both sets of 'scene windows.' He looked around to see Dr. Blackwell, smiling like a papa holding a newborn babe. He turned to look over his shoulder to see the two men sitting in the back of the room. He motioned them over as he came from around his desk. All four men sat together in a circle, kinda like a group therapy session.

"How do you feel, Scott?"

"Good. Great. Rested, actually."

Then he turned to the two guests. "Gentlemen. Did anything sound familiar?"

The thin older man spoke first. "Well, his first impressions seemed to be about me," he said. "I used to own a hardware store. I remember opening day and making my first sale. I was proud of that store."

"The images were fairly accurate?"

"More than that," he said. "They were spot on. The second image," he paused and took a deep breath. "That was accurate, too."

Scott sat forward to hear the thin man clearly. He spoke softly.

"My wife of fifteen years died about thirty years ago. She was all I had. We had no children. Cancer took her and most of my savings. I had to sell my store. I remember her funeral like it was yesterday," he said with a slight tremor in his voice.

"Thank you, Mr. Watkins," Dr. Blackwell said. "Mr. Kimball?"

The younger man sat up straight. "That was amazing," he said. "The first three stories seem right-on accurate. I remember rescuing the little boy." Then, as an after-thought, "How did you know I was a firefighter?" he asked Scott.

"I'm sorry. I didn't know that. Not before now," Scott said.

"You told him, didn't you?"

The doctor just shook his head.

"Wow. Like I said, I rescued that kid in one of my first fires. That was very realistic."

Dr. Blackwell looked like he had just received the Nobel Prize.

"Last summer my wife and I, and yes, I met her in the bar you described, we went to the Grand Canyon. I've never been to a more beautiful place."

Scott looked at Dr. Blackwell and half-expected him to jump up and high five him.

"But the other two—the church fire and the hospital or retirement home or whatever that place was, I've never been there. Those must have been from someone else."

"Interesting," Dr. Blackwell said. "Scott, perhaps you're recalling another vision you had recently?"

Scott shook his head. "I don't remember," he said.

With that, Dr. Blackwell called the gathering to a close. Both men said they'd gladly bring others to have "readings" with Scott and suggested he might get rich if he wanted to charge.

After they left, Dr. Blackwell turned to Scott. They talked about the meeting and Scott's successful ability to relive their experiences. Scott bounced on his toes as he walked out of Dr. Blackwell's office. He had it. He really had it! Now, if he only knew what it was.

***

Scott found it impossible to hold it in. Grace was already home when he arrived. He floated into the kitchen where she prepared supper and hugged her from behind, dancing around the kitchen floor and nibbling on her neck. She turned around in his arms and welcomed him home with a deep kiss.

"It was incredible," he said, pulling away. "Blackwell had two guys there I've never seen before and I saw visions from their past! I read them like a book! They were more clear than any of the dreams and hallucinations I've had in the past. This is a lot better than reality TV."

"Reality TV is not that good, anyway," Grace said.

"Yeah," Scott answered. "Bad analogy. But it

was like I was there. I lived those experiences." He felt alive, as if he were just coming out of a coma.

"And they all were true?"

"Well, all but two. We didn't have an explanation for that. But those guys were flabbergasted. One guy was a firefighter and I had visions of him fighting fires and taking a vacation and meeting his wife. I had never met him before and didn't know what he did. The other guy once owned a hardware store and I saw his grand opening."

"What kind of drugs did he give you?"

"Nothing. It was harmless. Something called Alprazolam."

"Hmmm. We use it at times at the hospital, but usually in small doses," Grace said. "You could probably get the same relaxing feeling after smoking a good joint."

"Doc said it was a small dose. Don't worry." He stared into her deep brown eyes.

"I'm glad you had a good day," Grace said. "I'm fixing tacos. Wanna help?"

"Tacos," Scott said. "We should go out for steak and champagne. I feel great!"

"Seriously?"

"Let's do it."

Grace removed her apron and headed back to the bedroom to change clothes. Scott followed her, jabbering about his session with Dr. Blackwell.

"I'm still concerned about the meds."

"Oh, it's fine. Dr. Blackwell says it's okay. We ought to take this on the road," Scott said. "We could make millions!"

"Slow down there, Houdini," Grace said. "One day at a time." She slipped out of her jeans and sweatshirt and in a matter of moments wore a nice dress, heels, and pearl earrings. She splashed on some perfume and the scent filled the room.

Scott watched her as she brushed her hair in front of the mirror and decided to try his own experiment. As he watched, he tried to relax and let visions of Grace come into his mind. He waited. Nothing. He tried harder to relax his mind. Still nothing.

"What are you doing?" Grace asked as she stepped away from the dresser.

"I'm just relaxing."

"Were you trying to read my visions?"

"Uh, no."

"Listen buster," she said walking over to where he sat on the bed. She stood between his spread legs and pulled him close to her. "If there's anything you want to know about my past, my life, my experiences, all you have to do is ask. I'll tell you. You don't need to read me."

He kissed her lips. "Got it." He pulled her down on top of him and pressed his lips to hers, feeling like a teenager dating the prom queen.

"We should hurry or we'll have to wait in line at the restaurant."

"It's okay," he said. "I'll wait in line. But I won't wait for this." He began to slide her skirt up so he could reach her.

"If this is one of the side effects of your medication, I suggest you take more," Grace said as she raised her hips to allow him to tug her panties off.

When they walked through the kitchen to the back door, Grace noticed something was missing. "Gumby? Gumby?"

The boxer slinked around the corner on soft feet, looking as guilty as a kid in a candy shop when the owner was gone. His ears laid flat against his head which hung low. "Did you eat the hamburger?" Graced asked the guilt-stricken dog.

"What? A whole pound of burger?"

Gumby turned around and went back into self-imposed isolation in the living room.

They both chuckled as they headed out the backdoor.

***

It now all began to make sense. Past images, events, visions that had tortured Scott became clearer.

As it does when you're in college, time had passed much too fast. Grading periods came and went and his parents seemed pleased with the scores. Grace came to visit the Moores for the Thanksgiving of Scott's junior year and in the early spring he proposed.

They planned a summer wedding soon after he graduated. Grace, who had taken a job at a local hospital spent most of her time planning for the big event and Scott spent most of his time in her apartment. Julie would be the Maid of Honor and Scott's geeky roommate would be the Best Man. Gowns and tuxedoes were chosen, a church reserved, invitations were mailed and Scott and

Grace awaited the approaching date.

One day while prepping for finals in his room, the hall payphone rang, snatching his attention away from his org. dev. textbook. Scott hustled through the door and stuck the black handle to his ear. A coed he barely knew shouted hysterically over the phone, mumbling something about Julie and Zombie Coffee. An icy chill slid down his back. He felt light-headed, as if he'd had a beer or two or three late at night.

He started running, again, out the door and across the quad toward the Zombie Coffee Shop. A battered, mangled wheelchair lay in the grass just beyond the crosswalk. Something dark and gooey covered the asphalt, staining the white crosswalk stripes. Students mingled with shoppers and shop owners to gape and stare.

Scott felt nausea creep inside his gut that threatened to explode from his throat. His hands began shaking. He knew inside what had happened. He somehow saw it in a dream or a hallucination or some sort of strange phenomenon. A sense of emotional grief mingled with guilt covered him. He would never see his friend, Julie, again. He could have prevented this if he'd just warned her.

Then he saw Grace. She sat alone on a nearby bench. Books were splayed on the ground around her. She cradled her face in her hands and sobbed uncontrollably.

Scott knew he couldn't worry about his own feelings since she was so immersed in her grief. He suppressed them to help her. Ignoring the cold stares of bystanders, he sat beside Grace and covered her in his arms. She shifted her position, lifting her face from her hands, and buried it in Scott's shoulder. Her arms wrapped around his neck in a vice grip. Scott started to cry, couldn't stop the rush of emotions, for his own loss, but also out of deep empathy for Grace.

They must have stayed like that for half an hour. People moved on. Someone sprayed down the blood stains in the street. Life kept going. At least, for them.

Scott stood up, gathered her books, and took Grace back to his dorm.

***

Dinner was at The Stone Tavern, an enchanted restaurant filled with soft lighting and fragrant smells of steaks cooking over charcoal flames.

"To an incredible future," Scott said, raising his glass of wine. "I can see it today."

Grace held her glass with a smile and tapped it to his. Then her smile changed.

"Scotty," she began. "There's something that has been bothering me."

"What? This thing has such amazing potential…"

"Yes, but what if something goes wrong. What if there are side effects."

"The tests are going great. There are no side effects."

"Not yet. Scotty, I love you dearly, but I would die if something bad happened to you."

"What could go wrong. Dr. Blackwell knows

what he is doing. He's a professional and…"

"What if he isn't giving you Xanax, but something else? Maybe the medication causes hallucinations."

Grace was playing nurse again—Nurse Nervous Nelly anxious and cautious.

"They're not hallucinations. They're actual visions…of peoples' lives. We've shown that."

"I don't know. I need to be sure you are safe."

"Okay," Scott said. "If I could get a pill to you, could you have someone at the hospital test it?"

"I don't know. Maybe. Dalman, one of the lab techs. He could probably do that."

"Then, that's the plan. I'll pick a slow day and fool the doctor into thinking I took a tablet. Then, maybe fake a vision or two and complain of a migraine. You can take the medication to Dalman for testing."

"I think we should go to the police," Grace said. "Dr. Blackwell may be dangerous."

"My visions certainly won't hold up in court. Just a little longer. If the pill is fake we can take this case to the police."

"Okay," Grace said. "This whole thing frightens me."

"Yeah," he said. "Me, too."

"I just don't trust him."

"Which brings up one more thing I've gotta do," Scott said, rubbing his chin.

"I think you're enjoying this so much you don't want to let it go."

Scott sat up straighter, surprised Grace would challenge him like that. "That's not true. I have no reason to risk my life for this study."

"Then what are you going to do, Scotty?"

"I've gotta get inside Dr. Blackwell's head."

***

A couple of days later, Scott got a break. Dr. Blackwell had just given him his pill for the morning. Scott fetched a cup of water from the water cooler and came back into the office sipping from the cup.

"What are we doing today?" Scott asked.

"I thought we might do some random readings," the doctor said.

Scott feigned illness. "So you don't have a formal test today? I'm fighting a bear of a headache."

"Really? Let me take a look." Blackwell took a small light and studied each of Scott's pupils, one at a time. Then he slipped a digital thermometer into Scott's mouth and jotted down the findings. "Doesn't look like you have a cold."

"Yeah. I just didn't sleep well last night," Scott said. "Grace had a movie on and it kept me awake."

"Oh, which one?"

"One of those SAW films," Scott lied and regretted not choosing a better movie title before the meeting.

"I wouldn't think of Grace as a slasher fan."

"She usually isn't. She just stumbled onto this one and we couldn't turn it off. It kinda freaked me out."

"I can imagine," the doctor said. "Have you

taken the Alprazolam, yet?"

"Yeah," Scott lied, again. He could feel the tiny pill in the palm of his hand. He worried that he might sweat and cause it to melt. "I just gulped it down."

After a moment of thought, Dr. Blackwell said, "All right. You'd better wait here at least an hour, to let the effects wear off. I don't want you driving right after taking a tablet."

"Okay, Doc," Scott said.

"You can relax on my sofa if you wish," Blackwell said. He retrieved a jacket from a coat rack in one corner of the room. "Elizabeth," he called to the receptionist. "I'm going to run downtown for a bit. I shouldn't be more than a couple of hours."

"Yes, sir," she called back.

Scott laid back as instructed. He raised his head from the arm of the sofa to look about the room. When he was sure he was alone, he shoved his hand into the pocket of his jeans and let the pill slip out from his palm. Then he removed his hand and crossed his arms over his chest. He closed his eyes.

Daily doses of the medication had made him more tired than usual. He found he napped more than before, often in the early afternoons. Even though he had not taken the pill today, he did feel tired. He welcomed the coming rest.

He woke with a start a bit later. Looking at his watch, he saw two hours had passed. He shook off the sleep and rose from the couch, a bit wobbly. Grabbing his coat, he wished Elizabeth a good afternoon, bounded out the door, and headed for the hospital.

Grace met him outside the emergency entrance. She took the pill and then kissed him on the cheek and told him she'd let him know what she found out when she got home.

Four hours later, Grace walked in the door and announced, "Alprazolam, prescription quality. Twenty milligrams."

"There was nothing unusual about the tablet?"

"Dalman said it contained traces of human sweat, but otherwise it was a prescription drug."

"So, what's that tell us?"

"Sounds like the visions are real and the drug is a catalyst, just as Blackwell said. I don't know whether to feel relieved or scared," Grace said.

"Both."

CHAPTER SEVEN

The next week was filled with breakthroughs, each better than the other.

On Monday, before the test began, Dr. Blackwell explained that it was important that Scott touch each person he was about to read. "Physical contact, of some sort, is critical. It's obviously not important to touch an individual through the entire event. A single touch will do."

Three subjects came into the room and Scott chose a middle-aged housewife over a soccer mom and Dr. Blackwell's temporary receptionist. He touched her elbow as if to guide her to her seat. She was an interesting read. He saw her wedding to a short man with an already-receding hairline and the weddings of her three daughters, each to men shorter than they. Scott had one false vision, as they had chosen to call them, with the woman. He saw her as a young woman at a book signing, autographing copies of a novel. It turned out she had never published anything.

"And did you see anything from the other

women in the room?" Dr. Blackwell asked.

Scott shook his head.

"Well I, for one, feel cheated," the soccer mom said, arms across her chest.

On Wednesday, they had lunch at China Pearl, a popular and crowded restaurant down the road from the doctor's office. Scott popped a pill, walked about the restaurant, bumping into several people as he had been instructed, and fifteen minutes later told tale after tale of one diner after the other. One man had received an Eagle Scout award. Another was arrested for embezzlement. A woman's visions included a ménage à trois with another woman and a man. One woman vacationed with what appeared to be her family in Hawaii. Scott caught a street sign for Honolulu.

Dr. Blackwell admitted that they had no way of verifying any of those visions, but pointed out that it was important to be able to choose visions from a large selection of people.

Scott gave the doctor a sly look and then said, "Watch this." He marched to the Boy Scout's table. Squatting down, he asked, "Excuse me. You look very familiar. Have we met?" He reached out his hand and shook the man's. "I'm Larry Sanger."

"Hi, Larry," the man said, shocked look on his face. "I don't recognize you..."

"I know," Scott interrupted. "Scout camp. I remember you from scout camp."

"Camp Woodruff?" Confusion on his face morphed into curiosity.

"Yeah!"

"Well, I'll be," the former scout said.

"Did you ever make Eagle?" Scott asked.

"Sure did. You?"

"Nah," Scott said. "I met girls my junior year of high school and dropped out."

"Do you know where other guys at that camp are? Jake? Greg?"

Scott begged off, saying something about the Army and returned to their table. "How's that for verifying a vision?"

"Impressive," Dr. Blackwell said.

"Yeah," Scott said, and slipped into silence. Something didn't feel right. He felt lewd, like he was snooping through a man's private photographs of his naked wife after a night of wild drinking. When he told Dr. Blackwell his feelings, the doctor just suggested that he enjoy the perks.

* * *

On Friday, they brought three subjects into the office who thought they were involved in a customer service experiment. Instead they tested Scott's ability to read others over distance.

"Where do you get these people?" Scott asked.

"Craigslist, mostly." Dr. Blackwell handed Scott another dose of Alprazolam.

Elizabeth escorted a man and two women into the office and everyone shared coffee and danish over light conversation for thirty minutes. Scott greeted each one with a smile and a warm handshake, careful to make physical contact in some way.

Then the doctor made the formal pitch. "Thank

you all for joining us today. I have a simple task for each of you. I will provide each of you with an address and some cash. I want you to go to that location and call my receptionist when you have arrived. Stay at that location for one hour, and then return here to complete a customer service survey."

Scott thought the survey was a lame ruse.

One by one the subjects accepted the envelopes and then left through the front door.

"Now Scott, I am trusting that you did not read anyone before they left."

"You have my word, Doc."

"I want you to read each person, even though they are quite some distance away from the office. Also, I'm going to record the session and let our guests view it when they return. Choose one vision for each person, but exercise discretion in your selection of events. I don't want to embarrass any of our volunteers." The comment seemed out of place for Dr. Blackwell, since he never seemed concerned about the feelings of others, before. Then he quipped with a peculiar smile, "At least not this time."

Within a half hour, everyone had called the office to let the doctor know they had arrived. Scott resumed his place in the arm chair and began to relax. Dr. Blackwell set up a video camera while Scott was preparing. When Scott relaxed, he pushed the record button.

An hour or so later, everyone returned.

"Thank you for your help today," Dr. Blackwell said. "Each of you will receive compensation when we dismiss in about an hour. In fact, your compensation will be double what you were promised."

No one objected, and they took seats around the office.

"I must confess," he added. "You were not selected for a customer service evaluation. That aspect of your instructions was a contrivance, if you will. I did that in an effort to ensure that the results and data are pure. The real purpose of this experiment was to test psychic ability over distance."

The man who looked older then the two women scoffed. "Are you serious?"

"I appreciate your skepticism," the doctor said. "Bear with me for a few moments, and I feel confident you'll all be pleased."

He directed them to turn their attention to the monitor hanging on the wall in the back of the room and pressed the play button on the video camera. "If anything you hear sounds familiar, please speak up."

Scott watched his image appear on the flat screen and grimaced. He looked older, ancient.

"Someone is making announcements on a P.A. System," on-screen Scott said. "I hear applause and I walk out onto a small stage. There's a fairly large crowd, mostly teenagers before me. Another announcement is made. I see the announcer. It's an older man, bald, wearing a suit. A young lady, looks like a high school senior, joins me on the stage. She's dressed in a formal gown."

Scott heard a gasp from one of the women in the room.

"More ladies join us. Another lady approaches with a silver crown—very ornate. Obviously, I'm in a coronation of some sort."

"Well that rules me out," the old man said.

"It's me!" a woman squealed. "I was queen of my high school prom."

On-screen Scott continued to describe the event, explaining how the person in the vision was crowned and the crowd cheered.

"That was over fifteen years ago," the woman said. "It was the best thing that happened to me in high school."

Dr. Blackwell paused the video playback and said, "Ms. Sherwood, you were situated three miles away at a coffee shop, am I correct?"

"That is right."

"Thank you," Dr. Blackwell said and pressed the play button on the camera.

On-screen Scott continued to describe his visions. "Okay, I'm selecting another story. I hear water, waves. I smell salty air. I'm standing next to a rail on a cruise ship. It's a large ship."

"I hate cruise ships," the old man said.

"It's me," the other woman said.

Scott's video image said, "We're pulling into port. The water is absolutely gorgeous—turquoise. We're still a ways from the dock."

Scott heard a sniff from the woman.

"I'm holding a vase with a top. No, it's an urn. The wind is blowing away from the ship and I open the top and pour the contents, a gray powder, out into the air. It's caught by the breeze and it spreads out over the water."

Dr. Blackwell paused the tape again. "Is that familiar?"

"Very," the woman whispered. She wiped an eye with a tissue. "My husband loved to vacation in St. Thomas. We must have taken ten cruises there. His last wish was that I would spread his ashes over the water."

"For the record," Dr. Blackwell said. "She was in the mall four miles away. Thank you."

"No, thank you," she replied. "It's a wonderful memory."

"Guess I'm next," the old man said.

"We'll see," He pressed the play button again.

Scott realized that the video was boring, on the surface. He was emotionless with little movement. But his words had power. "I must be in a hallway. I hear loud noises and echoes in here. Yeah. I'm in a long line. Soldiers. Everyone is dressed in military gear. Guy in front of me has a blond crew cut. Someone is yelling for us to pipe down." On-screen Scott grimaced and turned his head, as if not wanting to see something. "Someone just opened a door and the sunlight outside is blindingly bright. Now we're jogging, running through the doorway and out to an airport runway. We're all carrying duffle bags, but I can hardly feel the one over my shoulder."

On-screen Scott began to suck in air. "There's an airplane, a big, propeller plane, in front of us. We're heading for it. One by one we climb up the steps and into the plane."

Dr. Blackwell paused the recording once again. "Mr. Wright?"

97

The older man paused a moment, then said, "I can't deny it. I have to admit, I thought the other two of you were faking it. Like this was some set up. But, that was me, boarding a plane in the Philippines for 'Nam. I served there eighteen months."

"It sounded accurate?" Dr. Blackwell asked?

"Hell, yes. The kid in front of me, with the crew cut? He died in a grenade blast." Then, he said, "I was so scared that day, heading off to war, I almost pissed my pants. Sorry ladies."

"And you were in a sports bar, while Mr. Moore did his reading, right?"

"Yeah. Watching replays of weekend football."

"Well, I'd like to thank each of you for participating in this study. You can collect your payment at the door."

Each person stood to exit, but instead, they approached Scott one by one and thanked him.

"That was incredible," the first woman said.

"You are truly gifted," the other said.

"I've always been a skeptic," the man said. "But I'm a believer, now."

"Impressive," Dr. Blackwell said after everyone had left. "How do you feel?"

Scott thought for a moment to find the right word. "Humbled," he said.

***

Scott and Dr. Blackwell took some time away one morning and visited a coffee shop down the street in a quaint little brick building bordered by a consignment dress store on one side and a print shop on the other. The morning air was brisk, but not cool, and the tables outside on the sidewalk invited them to bask in the sun.

Sipping lattes and cappuccinos, they talked about how the study was progressing. Dr. Blackwell commented on the clarity of Scott's visions and how easily he had picked up the skill. He added that Scott had been able to focus on one certain person and exclude others, sounding like the professor he may have been. "What you are experiencing will shake the medical world, proving the existence of psychometry, the ability to know details about a person by simply touching them. Except, in your case, you can selectively screen out some people while focusing on the ones you want to read." Something in his voice, his tone, sounded as if such advances were trivial and well within his expectations.

Dr. Blackwell's view made sense to Scott. He mentioned that but also said the visions seemed to help some people. Most people seemed touched that others recognized, even validated their experience. Then there was Debbie, who was hurt by his comments.

The doctor brushed his words away with a wave of his hand.

"There is one thing that bothers me," Scott said.

"What's that?"

"It's the false visions. A few people didn't recognize a vision or two."

"Yes, I too have been concerned about them. But I remind you that they are rare. The literature, as you know, lacks a great deal on the subject of psychometry. Who knows why some are true and others are not. You know, even Babe Ruth didn't bat a thousand."

"What do you think causes them? They seem so real, just like the others."

Dr. Blackwell sighed, deep in thought, and chewed on the edge of his mustache. "We are treading in territory that has never been explored. Perhaps someone else's visions, perhaps mine, have bled over into your readings. You know how two radio stations that are close to each other on the dial sometimes bleed over into each other's bandwidth? Maybe that's what is happening."

Scott paused and let his analogy soak in.

"But then, on the other hand…"

Scott looked up from his coffee cup.

"From an entirely philosophical view, I have absolutely no proof in this hypothesis." The doctor began.

"What if the visions you see are not time-bound. That is, they are outside the bounds of our definition of time," sounding like a college professor again.

"Well how can I view them?"

"How could you view any episodes at all? It's a mystery. So why should we assume that viewing anyone's experience would fall into our concepts and definition of time."

"Okay," Scott said, but he felt he didn't understand everything he had heard.

"If the visions are not limited by time, then you could be seeing things in the past as well as things that have not happened, yet. Perhaps one of the reasons some of our subjects did not recognize certain events is because they will happen in the future…or may not happen at all."

"Then how can I see them?"

"You could if you captured events outside the dimension of time."

"Wow. That is heavy."

"Yes it is, isn't it?" He sipped on his cappuccino, looking like a blue ribbon winner at the science fair.

"So I'm telling the future?"

"The possible future, Scott," he said.

Scott paused in thought. "So perhaps fortune tellers in the past, you know, like gypsies, actually saw things that might happen in the future."

"Highly unlikely, but remotely possible," Dr. Blackwell said. "Remember, Dr. Dekhtyar created a drug that kick-started your abilities and those of your mother. The medication I have prescribed served as a catalyst, a booster, to make it easier to access these visions."

"Yeah, that's right."

"For a gypsy to tell the future, she or he would have to be genetically predisposed to do what Dr. Dekhtyar's drug did as well as what my prescriptions did. That seems a bit far-fetched."

"It all seems far-fetched," Scott said.

"I'm afraid the gypsies simply figured out a way to con people."

Scott sensed he was right. He wondered if Dr. Blackwell might have a bit of a con artist in him.

***

At the beginning of the week, Dr. Blackwell decided to try another type of remote viewing experiment. Scott downed an Alprazolam pill and a cup of water and sat opposite him at a table. One at a time, the doctor held up large, white, plastic-coated cards containing various symbols—squares, circles, triangles, stars and diamonds—that only he could see. He asked Scott to try to describe which card he held.

Scott gave it a shot, but couldn't see any of the symbols. His ability didn't work that way so he started guessing. Then he became bored, so he decided, on a whim, he would try to read Dr. Blackwell's visions. That turned out to be a little tricky because he had to read between guesses so the doctor wouldn't know what he was doing.

"I see a star," Scott said. Dr. Blackwell jotted something down in a notepad. Scott saw several stories as he read the doctor. He chose one and viewed a graduation ceremony.

He stood in line to walk across the platform to receive a diploma. As he reached for the scroll he noticed his sleeve contained three stripes—signs of a doctoral student.

"I think it's a square," he said. Again the doctor jotted something in his notebook.

Scott relaxed and continued to read Dr. Blackwell.

He saw someone come up to congratulate him. Scott didn't recognize the person but heard him call him by the name, "Dr. Blackwell..."

He backed out of that vision and into another.

Scott was there. He yelled something incoherent. The doctor was in a house that Scott didn't recognize. He shouted. He felt anger. "I'm not going to let you out of this so easily," he yelled. "I've invested a lot of effort and resources into this project and I'm not going to give up."

The doctor appeared to be talking directly to Scott.

He wondered if he was seeing a future event or one of the false visions.

"I don't care," Scott saw himself say. *"I don't want to do this anymore. You've been profiting from my abilities and it makes me feel shitty—like I'm doing something wrong."*

"You wouldn't even know you had these abilities if it weren't for me," Dr. Blackwell said. *"We're going to continue the study."*

"Scott? What symbol do you see?" the real Dr. Blackwell broke through the images. He was holding up another card.

"Oh, sorry." He rubbed his forehead with his fingers. "I think it's a square."

"You said, 'square' for the last three cards," Dr. Blackwell said.

"That's what I see." Sarcastically, he added, "Maybe you need a new set of cards."

Blackwell grimaced.

Then he heard himself say, "What you're doing is wrong. You've cheated people—blackmailed them. I'm going to the police."

"No," he shouted at Scott. He picked up a heavy object, a vase of some sort, and swung it in Scott's direction, striking him in the temple and knocking him against a nearby counter. Blood oozed from a gash in his head. "I've put years into this research." He swung at Scott again, knocking him to the floor. "You will not stop me."

"Scott?" the real Dr. Blackwell demanded. "What card am I holding now?"

"Uh, square, no. You've got a circle," Scott said.

"Hmmmm," the doctor responded.

In the vision Dr. Blackwell's hands trembled. He knelt by Scott and took a pulse. His heart beat slower than normal, but still strong. A sense of panic and desperation flooded over him. He couldn't let Scott go to the cops. He had to clean this mess up.

Reaching down, he opened Scott's mouth and poured several tablets from a prescription bottle into his mouth. He stood up and grabbed a whisky bottle from a nearby wet bar, screwed off the cap and poured the liquid after the tablets. If police found Scott's body, they'd assume he had overdosed and hit his head while falling.

"Scott," Dr. Blackwell said. "You don't seem to be taking this exercise seriously. What does the card say?"

In his vision he took a pillow from the couch and placed it over Scott's face. He pressed it down, forcing all of his weight on the pillow. The body beneath him began to squirm, to fight for life.

When the squirming stopped, Blackwell glanced in a mirror. Sweat poured from his balding head causing his glasses to slide down his nose. His steely goatee glistened from perspiration. He needed to get rid of the body...just in case.

After catching his breath, he bent over and picked up Scott's feet and dragged them toward the door, into the garage and to the rear of his Black BMW. He popped the trunk and hefted the body into the back.

After closing the trunk, he leaned back against the car, out of breath once again.

It took every ounce of Scott's will to keep from reacting to the vision he saw of Dr. Blackwell suffocating him. He inhaled like a diver preparing for an underwater swim. Try as he might to focus on the cards, he couldn't concentrate. Frustrated, scared, he broke off the exercise. Shaking his head, he said, "Dr. Blackwell. I can't. I'm just not feeling well today."

The vision had disappeared.

"Could we wrap this up? Maybe tomorrow."

"Certainly, Scott," Dr. Blackwell said. He stood up and gathered the cards and notepad and walked back to his desk. "Tomorrow, same time. All right?"

Scott stood. He nodded and wobbled toward the front door. "See you then," he said, not sure he ever wanted to see Blackwell again.

He left for home…and Grace.

CHAPTER EIGHT

The next week Dr. Blackwell invited Scott to attend a special dinner sponsored by a group of technology investors. They dined in an elegant restaurant in the business district. Scott had never been there and doubted he ever would go there again. His wallet couldn't afford the check and his diet couldn't take the rich cuisine. His idea of a nice dinner out was taking Grace to Qdoba for tacos.

The small dining room, separated from the main room by massive double doors, was decked out in ornate furniture. Paintings, no doubt originals, lined the walls. Scott felt out of place here, like a homeless guy in a fancy castle.

Most of the investors were much older than Scott and they all reeked confidence. Several smoked Cuban cigars, but Scott couldn't tell if they were for show, or if the executives in this room simply liked cigars. He sensed the former.

Scott and Grace seldom invested in the stock market. The Market was for people richer and smarter than he.

Since the reading in which the doctor violently killed him, he had been very guarded about where they met, watching the doctor warily at all times. He would agree to the coffee shop and to the doctor's office and to other public places. Everything else was out of bounds. Except this restaurant on this evening.

Less than fifteen people gathered at this exclusive event to meet with Gary Ross, CFO of Grabel Communication Technologies, a leader in the cellular phone industry. Grabel's stock had recently taken a hit in the market and Ross had forecast in the last quarterly call that the stock might suffer even lower returns.

Scott took one of Dr. Blackwell's pills, which the doctor kept in a prescription bottle in his jacket pocket, moments after they took their seats. Mr. Ross, a short, squat man wearing thick glasses and possibly the ugliest tie Scott had ever seen, entered the room and greeted each of the investors, one at a time. Scott made a special effort to shake hands with the executive.

During dinner Scott gave some thought to reading Dr. Blackwell again, but decided against it. It was best to stick to the plan, at least for the moment. A representative of the sponsoring investment group introduced Ross who spent a half-hour talking about the telecommunications industry, past advances, potential opportunities and a few juicy humorous stories about his experiences. He opened the floor to questions at the end of the talk, but vehemently declined to talk about specific expectations concerning the stock. The only thing he offered was, "I believe in our company. If I had a few bucks to spare," he said chuckling, "I'd put it in Grabel."

"Can you elaborate?" Dr. Blackwell asked.

"Well, now, I wouldn't want to violate any SEC legislation," Ross answered. "In fact, I wouldn't tell you we have some pending contracts in China and Brazil, nor that our competitors are struggling through serious manufacturing problems. I would never say that."

Murmurs rumbled around the table.

After the meeting was over, Dr. Blackwell led Scott out of the room with the rest of the investors. They moved down the street to a local bar where they found a table and sat down to debrief. Dr. Blackwell ordered a beer but encouraged Scott to avoid alcohol while on Alprazolam, so Scott drank a Pepsi.

Scott leaned back in his chair and forced himself to relax. Within a few moments, he said, "Okay. I'm ready."

"Tell me about Gary Ross," Dr. Blackwell said, almost giddy with excitement.

"He's been busy. There are lots of episodes to choose from. I hear music, Christmas music. There's a Christmas tree and presents. He's opening one and it's an electronics kit. No surprise there." He opened his eyes to see Dr. Blackwell rapidly typing on his Samsung phone.

Scott continued. "I hear a single voice. It's a man. He's speaking very steadily, like he's trying to make his voice neutral. He's saying Ross is a part of a reduction in force and describes the separation package. Looking around the room, there are Microsoft logos everywhere."

"Very good. Microsoft laid Ross off several years ago. Some sources said he never got over it and always resented Microsoft. Anything else?"

"Here's something. I hear excited voices. There's a clink of glasses and a fizzing sound. A man is pouring champagne. Someone in a three-piece suit says he's glad he had placed his stock order a couple of weeks earlier. Ross agrees and says he knew their stock would explode. He announces the name of someone in the room who won the office pool to come closest to the stock price at the closing bell. Everyone congratulates that man." Scott paused for a moment, enjoying the anticipation that came with making Blackwell wait. "After the employees left the office, he checks his portfolio on his phone. Apparently, Grabel stock had risen to over sixty a share."

"Very good. Tell me more."

"Ross is estimating he profited over eighteen million dollars in the stock purchase. He's laughing."

Dr. Blackwell touched Scott's hand, bringing him out of the vision state. The two men locked eyes and Dr. Blackwell mouthed the words, "Wait a moment."

A man wearing a handsome suit walked by within earshot of their table, sipping a drink with an umbrella in it. A few moments later, he walked to a table occupied by some ladies and began to talk with them.

"Go ahead," Dr. Blackwell said.

"That's about it."

"Can you tell the date?" Blackwell asked. Impatience lifted his voice. "After all, it may not be this quarter."

"Just a moment. There's a calendar on the Samsung screen. It says…three weeks from now."

"That's wonderful," Dr. Blackwell said. "Well done."

"There are other images," Scott offered. "One's a childhood memory. Another shows a wedding."

"No, I think we've seen enough for tonight. You need to go home and get some rest."

"Okay, Doc. Anything you say."

They drove home excited, talking about the visions and the special technique Scott was developing. Scott shared the enthusiasm, but with a measure of caution.

The house lights were off, so Scott entered his home quietly, as quietly as he could with a rambunctious boxer in the house. Gumby barked in a threatening tone until he saw Scott walk through the door. Then he resumed his wriggle position, bowing in the middle and dancing sideways as boxers are known to do. Scott spent a moment petting the enthusiastic dog and then turned to the second bedroom which he used as a home office. He switched on his laptop and checked the stock prices. Grabel was down to a five year low of thirty-nine dollars a share.

He switched off the computer and went to bed.

***

Upon entering the office, Elizabeth handed him a pill on a little tray and a note instructing him to read the Mayor.

"Scott," said Dr. Blackwell. "I'd like to introduce you to our mayor, Don Hill."

He had just walked into the doctor's office, as he did most mornings. Mayor Hill sat in Scott's usual chair.

"Hello, Mayor," Scott said, offering his hand.

The mayor half stood, reached out and shook Scott's hand and then sat back down, barely acknowledging his presence. His handshake was cold, clammy, and weak.

"Can we continue our conversation in private?" Mayor Hill asked.

"I apologize for interrupting," Scott said and quietly backed out the door.

After he closed the office door behind him, he settled into the couch in the outer office. The clicking sound of Elizabeth's computer keyboard had a lulling affect. He allowed himself to relax and then searched for the mayor's visions. The first shouldn't have surprised him, but it did.

Mayor Hill stood before an audience of high school students. An announcer introduced him as the president of the senior class. In another vision the mayor held the keys to a new Chevrolet Camaro. Continuing the search, *he passed a college graduation ceremony, the opening of a new ice factory, and the birth of a child.*

Then he found what he was looking for.

The mayor stood in a clearing in the woods before a naked, shivering boy, barely ten years old, and shouted, "Bobby Jacobs, you will do whatever I tell you to do and you won't tell anyone about this or I'll fire your daddy. Do you hear me?"

Scott quickly backed out of the lewd scene, feeling revulsion at the frightened look on the little boy's face. The reality, the harshness of the vision struck him like a freight train slamming into a school bus. He didn't have to see anymore. He knew what else happened in that wooded area.

The door to Dr. Blackwell's office opened and the doctor escorted the mayor to the front door.

"Think carefully about my offer," Mayor Hill said. "Your support is critical."

"I will be in touch with you," Dr. Blackwell said.

Scott followed the doctor back into his office.

"Did you read him? Did you find anything?"

"Yes, I did," Scott said. "I think I found what you're looking for."

Both sat down. "Tell me." He leaned forward, arms resting on his knees, which bounced enthusiastically.

"Mayor Hill used to own an ice factory, didn't he?"

"That's how he made his riches. He sold ice throughout the county and in surrounding counties."

"Find a man who works for him or used to work for him whose last name is Jacobs. He had a son named, Bobby." Scott paused a moment. "Hill molested Bobby."

"Are you sure? This isn't the sort of thing you'd

accuse someone of if you did not know for certain."

"I really don't want to see it again, but I can repeat the search," Scott said. "It happened once in a clearing in a wooded area. I don't know if there were other episodes. He threatened to fire Mr. Jacobs if Bobby told on him."

Dr. Blackwell jotted notes on a yellow pad of paper.

The rest of the day consisted of a basic recheck. The doctor drew Scott's blood for analysis. He administered several personality and psychological surveys. He interviewed Scott about his experience, his visions, and his behavior outside the office. All the time, Dr. Blackwell seemed antsy. He kept looking at the pad of yellow paper, as if he'd rather be dealing with something there than administering these tests.

Blackwell appeared pleased with Scott's progress and test results. Scott returned home with mixed feelings. On the one hand, he was pleased with his progress. Before meeting the doctor he had no idea of the potential he held. On the other, he feared he was destined to hurt and manipulate others.

The latter feeling far outweighed the former.

CHAPTER NINE

The next morning Scott warily returned to work at Dr. Blackwell's office. The doctor said he had a light schedule, so they thought they would do some road work, which was his way of saying they were going out for coffee.

Dr. Blackwell drove Scott to a little diner by the interstate highway. He said, "Scott, I want to go inside the restaurant, enjoy a cup of coffee or dessert, and then return to the office. From there, I would like you to read a person you saw in the diner."

"Sounds good," Scott replied. As long as they were in public, Scott felt safe.

The waitress greeted them at the table and presented each with laminated menus. She looked to be a woman who worked hard, keeping her frame thin because of her intense schedule and job. Scott imagined she had looked quite pretty a few years back. Now, traces of beauty lingered here and there, especially when she smiled.

Both men ordered coffee. Scott popped one of

the doctor's tablets with a gulp of water. The diner displayed a delectable golden brown apple pie in a glass box and neither could resist. Scott made a point to touch her hand lightly when she handed him his plate. He concentrated on the waitress—she had called herself Sherry. He also paid close attention to Dr. Blackwell. They finished the pie and coffee and Blackwell left a seventy-five cent tip. Scott tossed a couple of extra dollars on the table while Blackwell paid the bill.

Back at the office, Scott sat back in the armchair and began to relax. He skipped the images of Blackwell. He didn't care to see them, at least not now. Instead, he focused on Sherry.

"Okay. You know the drill. Tell me about the episodes," Dr. Blackwell said.

"That's odd," Scott said. "I usually see several stories to choose from. But this time, there is only one."

"Okay. Tell me about that one."

Scott moved forward into that image. "I hear music. Loud music. Not rock and roll. At least not real rock and roll. It's high school band music. They're playing Chicago's "Twenty-five or Six to Four." Not bad, but not great."

He heard Dr. Blackwell chuckle.

"She's playing a trumpet, in an auditorium, no, a band shell. The director is conducting very intensely. He seems determined to get the best out of the band."

Everyone stopped playing. They began packing up their instruments.

"The concert, performance or whatever it was is over. Sherry moves to the back of the audience and sits on a folding chair watching other bands."

Scott looked about the audience into a sea of young teenage faces.

"The announcer is recognizing different groups. I guess it's a competition. Yes, he says it's the Mississippi State Band Competition. He's announcing the number one band for the year...the year 1976. Apparently the winner is Sherry's high school. All of the students around her are screaming. Wait. The director just pointed at her. I think Sherry was the captain or president or something because she is now running down the aisle and up to the stage. She's presented with a large trophy. Everyone is cheering."

"Okay," Blackwell said. "Back out of that episode. "Are there still no other episodes?"

"Nope. That's the only one." Scott opened his eyes.

"Strange." It's a shame we didn't hire her so we could ask further questions. He made a note in his pad. "It's odd that she did not have more episodes."

"Then again, Doc. I never see every incident of a person's life. I just see certain scenes."

"Well, I think that's enough for the day. I'll see you again tomorrow morning."

Scott excused himself and hurried home. When he burst in to the house, he surprised Gumby who was sleeping on the living room sofa, an area forbidden to him. The wily dog approached Scott as if he was apologetic and excited at the same time.

"Not now, Gumby," Scott said and the dog

slinked away into the back of the house.

He fetched a tape recorder, checked to see the tape and batteries were new and sat down in his easy chair. He turned the recorder on and allowed himself to relax. "Okay. I can see all of the images of people I've touched this morning. Sherry, the waitress is still there."

The dog interrupted him by running into the room and pressing his nose against Scott's shoe. Apparently, he heard Scott talking and assumed he was calling Gumby in for some back-scratching. Scott ignored the dog and he eventually went away.

"I see the images for Blackwell. I'm moving forward to them. I see the two images I read last week—the one of his doctoral graduation and the one where he killed…me." He felt odd saying those words out loud. "There are other scenes. I'm moving to one, now. It seems like a formal meeting. Two or three people are in a business office, no, a law office. Oh, it's the reading of a Will. Aaaah, apparently, Blackwell is the benefactor of a good deal of money, bequeathed to him from his father. Interesting."

Scott didn't feel there was anything of value there.

"I'm moving back out of that scene. Here's another. Hmmmm. Apparently, Dr. Blackwell is being recognized for some research. They called it a, 'Psychometric Viewing Study.' From the way he's moving, I sense that he is old, maybe in his seventies. The skin on his hand looks old. The bastard must have cashed in on his research with me."

"Now I'm checking out another scene. I hear someone talking. He's animated. Now I see him. It's Mayor Hill. He's threatening Dr. Blackwell, but the doctor is telling the mayor to sit down. Now he's describing the incident about young Bobby Jacobs."

Scott saw the mayor's face turn ashen. He heard Dr. Blackwell tell the mayor that he had signed statements from Robert Jacobs and he was willing to release them to Bobby's father and to the public.

"He's blackmailing Mayor Hill for two hundred thousand dollars," Scott said.

He backed out of that image and entered the next one—the last one for Dr. Blackwell. "I hear outside noises. The doctor is sitting with me at the coffee shop down the road from his office. It looks to be late in the morning. The cars driving by are current models, so this must be around the present time. I'm looking for a date. Wait, the waitress just brought the doctor's credit card receipt. I see him signing it. The date is October 15, five days from now. We're walking away from the coffee shop. The doctor is in front of me."

Scott heard tires squeal before he saw the Jeep turn the corner. The doctor was looking the other way, over his shoulder, away from traffic. Through the doctor's eyes, he turned toward the sound just in time to see a beige Jeep collide with him and roll over his body. Scott felt nauseous. Pain rushed through him. "Dr. Blackwell has been hit. No, he's

119

been run over by a car. I see myself leaning over his body. He is badly injured."

Scott felt like half of his face was on fire–as if it was scraped away.

"I hear the sounds of sirens. People are running from the diner and from the shops. A young man is throwing up by the lamppost. It looks like someone is getting out of the Jeep. It's a woman. She's talking on a cell phone. I think it was an accident."

The images began to dissolve, like a sugar cube in water. The visual scene slowly faded into white emptiness. Voices and street noise could still be heard for a bit. Then, the noise faded as well.

Scott found himself outside the images, looking in. His hands were shaking. He forced himself to wake up.

"I just saw Dr. Blackwell's death," he said into the tape recorder. "I don't understand how that can be since I also saw him receive a special award at a very old age." He paused the tape to consider what he'd just said. His shirt was sticking to the sweat on his underarms. "It was very real, just like the other images. Something happened. Dr. Blackwell will be run over by a car in five days."

"Unless I stop it."

***

"Scotty, are you all right?"

"I'm fine, Grace," he said. "When you get a

moment, come talk with me." Gumby lay on the floor beside him in his easy chair. The only light came from the hallway.

Grace came straight into the living room and sat on the sofa. "What's going on? Why are you sitting in the dark?" Wrinkles furrowed her brow. She smelled of antiseptic.

"I told you I had to get inside Blackwell's head, right?"

"Yes, you did," she said. "Did you?"

"I did."

"What did you see?" Grace asked as if she really didn't want to know. "I know he is a horrible man."

"No. Nothing like that," Scott said, looking at his wife. "I've been trying to figure this whole thing out. Help me, here. Okay?"

"Okay." She moved to a hassock opposite him.

"For starters, it seems like my visions are real, right?"

"Well, most of them have actually happened," she said.

"And we know that the drug serves as some sort of a catalyst. It makes it easier for me to see the visions clearly."

"Add to that the fact that we know Dr. Blackwell has been giving you Alprazolam. Dalman confirmed that."

"Right. He's not feeding me a hallucinogen."

"I still wouldn't put it past him. He's an evil man," Grace said.

"The other night when Blackwell and I attended the Gary Ross dinner, I saw a vision in which Grabel stock had a huge jump in value. I'm sure

Blackwell is using the information I gave him for investment purposes."

"Wow," Grace said. "Insider information…"

"I'll give him this. He's a crafty son of a bitch."

"That crafty son of a bitch may kill you."

"Well, since I know what to expect, I'll guard against that. That's one vision that is destined to be a false one."

"It had better be," Grace declared. Grace was a determined woman. She could be very stubborn about a lot of things, but never as much as her relationship to Scott.

"Speaking of false visions, we know some of the visions aren't real, at least they aren't real, yet." Scott took another swig of the beer in his hands. "You might want one of these yourself," he said.

"Go ahead," Grace said.

"We had an easy day today," Scott said. "Blackwell let me off early. I came home and did my own session. I read him, right here in this chair."

"Was it as accurate? After all, you weren't right there with him."

"Yeah, it was accurate. I recorded the vision as I saw it. You can listen to it later."

Gumby got up, sidled over to Grace, and let her rub his ears. "Tell me about it, yourself," Grace said.

"I saw some of what I'd seen before. I saw Blackwell receive his doctorate. I saw the horrible scene where he killed me. I also saw an episode in which he received an award. In it he was an old man."

"Well, that could happen in the future," she said.

"I also saw him blackmail Mayor Hill," Scott said. "I read the mayor a week or so ago and I saw an episode where he molested a kid. Dr. Blackwell used that against the mayor for a couple of hundred grand."

"I told you he was slimy," Grace said. She leaned forward as if to sense more was to come.

"But then I saw a scene and I confirmed the date by looking at a restaurant receipt. It was five days from now. We were having tea at the shop near his office. I saw him starting to cross the street when a Jeep turned the corner, ran over him, and he died." Scott felt odd describing it so objectively. He could tell Grace was assimilating this.

"Oh, my God. How do you know he died."

"I saw the accident. I felt pain. And, it ended different than the others. It all sort of faded away."

"You're certain of the date."

"Yeah. Next Tuesday. And, I was there. I saw myself watching the vehicle turn the corner before hitting him."

Both sat silently for a long while. Gumby broke the silence by shaking his head violently from side to side, something he did when he woke up and after his ears were scratched sufficiently.

"The question is…" Scott breathed. "Do I try to stop it?"

Grace took a deep breath. "Can you tell him you read him and saw him die?"

"He'd be pissed that I read him. I've seen him when he's pissed. Not a pretty sight."

Grace stood up. "Let it happen. We don't need

anything else from him. Let him walk right in front of that car and send his miserable soul to Hell. Remember, you saw him take your life."

"If I kept silent, wouldn't it be the same as killing him myself?" Scott asked.

"He deserves it."

"I'm not a killer. If I do that, am I any better than he is?"

"You're not Paul Blackwell," Grace said, pulling her husband closer to her. She moved to the arm of the lounger and poured herself onto him. "You never could be."

"But shouldn't I try to prevent it?"

"Why?"

"Because he has a life. A soul."

"That's questionable," she said. After a moment of thought she added, "Then, don't stop it, but make sure you don't allow it either. You said you were there in the vision, right?"

"Yeah."

"Well, next week take him somewhere else. Stay in the office. Call in sick. Tell him you're going to stay home. If you're not there, you can't blame yourself if he lives or dies, right?"

"Maybe." He stared at the floor and shook his head slowly.

"Well?"

"What if I want him to die?"

CHAPTER TEN

On Tuesday Scott called the office early and feigned sickness. He even sniffed out loud once or twice and faked a cough to add reality to his phone call. The receptionist took his message and promised to pass it along to Dr. Blackwell.

Concerned that the doctor might call to check on him, Scott took Gumby for a morning walk. The sidewalk was fairly busy with soccer moms and would-be athletes exercising their way to healthier lives. As he passed each person, Scott felt completely disconnected from the world around him. They moved about their lives, exercising, going to work, going shopping, oblivious to the devastating event that would occur later that day. He, on the other hand, knew that a man may very well be run over by a Jeep in just a matter of hours and he chose to do nothing about it. He surprised himself when he said aloud, "Murder by omission? Is that possible? Is that sin?"

It was enough to make a monk lose his faith. His head hurt. Nerves bounced on his fingertips.

Despite Gumby's resistance, Scott turned around half-way through their usual walk and headed home.

Grace was at the hospital, too busy, no doubt, to offer advice. Scott stripped off his sweats and climbed in the shower hoping the hot, sudsy water might wash his guilt down the drain. It didn't work.

He ate a late breakfast and thumbed through the newspaper. As usually, nothing inside interested him. He looked at his watch. Nine thirty. He went outside, gathered his leaf blower, and blew some leaves into tiny piles. At nine fifty, he went back inside and tried to read a book. Ten minutes later he poured another cup of coffee.

Finally, he determined to find out if the vision would come true. He pulled on a jacket and drove downtown. Leaves were whirling about the parking places surrounding the public garden that lay across the street from the used clothing store. He chose one of the leaf-strewn spaces. From here, he could see the fatal corner where his vision had sentenced Dr. Blackwell to his death. The window of the coffee shop gave off a glare and Scott couldn't tell if Dr. Blackwell was inside or not. He wished, prayed, hoped the doctor had chosen not to come out for tea by himself this morning.

As if to disconfirm his thoughts, the wooden door to the coffee shop swung open with a ring of a bell and the doctor stepped outside. Scott's heart fell to his gut. It was going to happen. He had to stop it.

He opened the driver's door just as a truck sped by, horn honking. He pulled the door shut quickly, narrowly missing the truck. The near-accident left him shaking like one of the leaves on the trees around the park. He checked for traffic, opened the door again, and looked for the doctor. He stood outside the coffee shop, smoking a cigarette. Scott watched in horror as he seemed to take note of something across the street and began walking toward it.

Scott sprinted in his direction, convinced he would walk into the path of the oncoming Jeep. A driver in a sport car yelled at Scott to get out of the street. "Dr. Blackwell," he called.

The man kept walking.

"Hey! Dr. Blackwell," he yelled again.

The doctor didn't stop, but looked over his shoulder to see who called as he stepped into the street. Just then, a Jeep, driver talking on her cell phone, swerved around the corner. Blackwell turned to face the Jeep and Scott watched in horror as the vehicle knocked him to the street and then bounced over his body.

Scott ran to the injured doctor and knelt down beside him. Blood pooled on the brick street beneath his body. Half of his face was left somewhere up the road, scraped away like earth moved by a bulldozer. Chunks of his goatee hung from his chin. His left eye hung half-out of its socket.

"Dr. Blackwell," Scott said. "Can you hear me?"

Blackwell opened his right eye and looked into Scott's. After a moment, a knowing look crossed his face. "You knew," he whispered. "You knew."

Scott looked up. The woman driving the Jeep

had pulled over and continued to talk on her cell phone, although much more hysterically. Others ran out of the coffee shop. "Call the police," someone yelled.

Scott turned back to the doctor, who began to spit great globs of blood out of his ravaged mouth. Instinctively, Scott reached down into his jacket pocket and retrieved the bottle of Alprazolam. He unscrewed the top and discretely popped one of the pills.

Within moments, he had entered the doctor's thoughts and was exploring his stories. He tapped into the one in which the doctor crossed the street in the path of the oncoming Jeep. Again he saw the accident. Nothing had changed. The image began to blur, to fade. Compelled, he stayed with the doctor. He wanted, had to see the final vision.

In a flash, all of the visions came at him, one by one, until the last one passed. Missing was the vision of Dr. Blackwell receiving the prize as an old man, as if it had never happened, for it never had. Also missing was the episode in which Blackwell killed Scott.

The ambulance arrived and paramedics moved Scott away so they could attend to the body.

Scott looked into the doctor's face and saw he was dead. He pocketed the pill bottle and walked away, toward the park, to a green bench where he slumped down to rest, exhausted. Somehow he had just experienced death and lived. Not any death, but one he played a part in. His gut felt weak, his stomach churning. He knew he would throw up.

An old lady, perhaps in her eighties walked up the sidewalk leaning heavily on her cane. She looked up toward the crowd gathering around the accident. Paramedics loaded the body into the back of the ambulance and left police to disperse the crowd.

"May I join you?" the old lady asked.

Scott nodded.

She sat down beside him. "Oh, my," she said. "That doesn't look good."

"No, it doesn't," Scott said.

"Did you know the man?"

Scott nodded.

"Was he a good man?" she asked.

Scott paused. As many hours as he had spent with Dr. Blackwell over the last few weeks, he couldn't honestly answer the question without some consideration. He thought long and hard, searching for the answer. He thought about the blackmail effort with the mayor. He thought about how he manipulated the stock market. He thought about the image of Dr. Blackwell hitting him with a vase. Finally, he shook his head. "No, he wasn't."

The lady seemed to take in what Scott said and process it. Then, she leaned forward on her cane and pulled herself into a standing position. "That's too bad," she said and resumed her walk up the sidewalk. "Such a waste."

Scott remained in his place, sitting on the park bench and watching the police as they worked with the crowd, asking questions and taking notes. He had failed. He had not prevented the doctor from dying, although he wasn't sure that he should have tried. The facts crept into his consciousness. Dr. Blackwell had died. He would never again offer anything to the world. His presence, his essence, his influence, was gone, forever.

***

He had finished off a bottle of Jack when Grace parked in the garage and hustled through the back door.

"Hi, Gracie," Scott called through slurred speech. He knew she hated seeing him in this condition, but there was no way in Hell he would care.

"What happened?" she demanded.

"Blackwell died," he announced.

"How do you know?"

"I saw it happen." He heard his voice slur the "S" and made no attempt to speak clearly.

"Are you all right?"

"I'm fine," he said. "Me and Gumby." he reached for the dog lying beside him, but Gumby lay too far away. He looked like he was swatting at imaginary flies.

"Did you give Gumby whisky again, tonight?"

"He took it from me," Scott announced.

"Well, I'll have to talk with Gumby about that," Grace said.

"He's a bad dog."

"Scott," Grace said.

"Yep?"

"How did Dr. Blackwell die?"

Scott paused a moment and then looked down at the floor. Her question made him deal with the reality of the incident, something the whiskey kept him from doing. "Just like I saw it in the dream," he said. "He stepped in front of a Jeep."

Then he held up a bottle of pills. "I've got the magic seeds."

"What?"

"Took them out of his pocket," Scott said.

Grace took the pills.

"Well," she said. "I think you need to stay here with Gumby and sleep it off." She pulled a blanket from the sofa and covered his legs with it. "When you're ready, come to bed."

"Otay," he said and waved goodbye.

***

Scott slept in as long as he could. Eventually, he had no more sleep in him and he just lay in bed trying not to think about visions, the doctor, or the future. But try as he might, he couldn't stop the thoughts. Stressful times did that to Scott. Grace had warned him about dwelling on frightening events.

Dr. Blackwell was dead. Scott didn't hear anything about the funeral. He assumed it was held somewhere else, far away. Eventually he rolled out of bed, stepped over his sleeping dog and wandered into the kitchen to find something to consume for breakfast. Grace had left a note saying she had gone grocery shopping to pick up some miscellaneous items.

After slapping some peanut butter onto burned toast, he leaned back against the kitchen counter and savored his brunch creation. A stack of mail Grace had brought in earlier lay near the sink. He thumbed through the letters and came upon an envelope addressed personally to him, in plain print. There was no return address. The postmark was smudged, but looked like it came from Pennsylvania. Scott tore the envelope open and pulled a couple of sheets of paper from inside. Three photographs slipped through his fingers and fell to the floor. He knelt down and retrieved the pictures and thumbed through them as he stood back up. He froze.

The pictures were of him. Try as he might, he couldn't recognize the location of the first one. In it he was dressed in ski gear, cap with goggles on the top, bibs, and scarf. He held ski poles in each hand. A magnificent mountain view of a ski run cascaded behind him. The photo confused him. He had never visited that ski slope. As a poor skier, the moguls behind his photo would have killed him.

The second photo showed Scott posing in front of the Eifel Tower. It couldn't have been long ago—maybe a year or two. Crowds wearing current fashions milled along the streets in the background.

The third photograph could have been taken yesterday. He was dressed casually in a t-shirt and jeans. He stood in someone else's kitchen, washing dishes next to an attractive lady about the same age. Scott had never seen the appliances on the kitchen counter behind the couple or the lady in the photo. It was as if he had a second life. Strange.

He picked up the sheet of paper and read the printed words.

Hello.

My name is Martha. I am sending this letter to you with profound sadness and a strong request that you do not contact me. My life has been threatened by a man named Paul Blackwell. If he finds out that I have contacted you, I am sure he will kill me.

For forty-three years I was mother to the young man in the photographs. His name is Kevin. He was a salesman, a husband and a wonderful, compassionate American. That is, until Paul Blackwell found him and brainwashed him into believing he had extraordinary powers. Dr. Blackwell confused him, drugged him, and used him to con others to pay him large amounts of money. Kevin died just over a year ago. The authorities said he committed suicide.

I should mention that we adopted Kevin when he was an infant. After his death, I did a great deal of personal research. My adoption agency said he was born in Latvia and that he had a twin brother—you.

I believe that Paul Blackwell may have reached out to you and am writing to warn you that he will lie, cheat, and manipulate you in every way imaginable. He is a despicable man. Do not trust him. Do not believe his lies. Stay away from him.

Again, I urge you not to contact me. I know Dr. Blackwell will kill me if you contact me.

−Martha

The second page consisted of a photocopy of a newspaper clip, heavily marked with a black pen. It was an obituary from a local newspaper.

Former ▮▮▮▮▮▮▮▮▮▮ *resident and regional sales director Kevin* ▮▮▮▮▮▮▮▮▮▮ *died on February* ▮▮▮▮▮▮▮▮▮. ▮▮▮▮▮▮▮▮▮▮. *He was forty-three years old and had moved from* ▮▮▮▮▮▮▮▮▮▮ *in 2000.*

Born November 17, 1963, he was a longtime employee of ▮▮▮▮▮▮▮▮▮▮. *As a young person, he was elected president of his high school debate team. He was an Eagle Scout. He loved to play golf and fish. He graduated cum laude from* 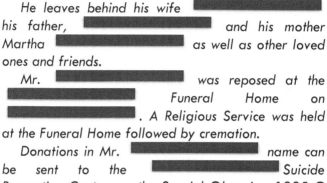 *University and married his college sweetheart in 1991.*

He will be remembered as a loving husband, son, and friend with a wide smile and jovial sense of humor. He showed compassion to everyone.

He leaves behind his wife ▮▮▮▮▮ *his father,* ▮▮▮▮▮ *and his mother Martha* ▮▮▮▮▮ *as well as other loved ones and friends.*

Mr. ▮▮▮▮▮ *was reposed at the* ▮▮▮▮▮ *Funeral Home on* ▮▮▮▮▮ *. A Religious Service was held at the Funeral Home followed by cremation.*

Donations in Mr. ▮▮▮▮▮ *name can be sent to the* ▮▮▮▮▮ *Suicide Prevention Center, or the Special Olympics, 1225 G Street, NW, Suite 500, Washington, D.C. 20005-3140.*

Scott leaned back against the kitchen counter and stared at the opposite wall, letting the words in the letter soak in. He had a twin brother.

Grace pushed the back door open and charged into the kitchen carrying two handfuls of plastic bags. She hefted them onto the kitchen counter.

"Hi, hon," she said, pecking him on the cheek. "Are you okay? You look pale."

"Aren't you going to ask if I've seen a ghost?"

"I was getting to that."

"I did." Scott handed her the photographs.

"When were these taken, dear? Where were you?"

Scott locked Grace's eyes with his own. "They aren't pictures of me. They are of my twin brother."

Bewilderment, followed by shock and then surprise covered her face. "Is that true?"

Scott handed her the letter. She read it while backing up to the kitchen table. Without looking, she dragged out the chair and sat down. She read the obituary. Then she picked up the pictures again. "These are incredible," she said. "He looks so much like you."

"That's what they say about twins."

Scott pulled a bottle of water out of the refrigerator and took the chair opposite Grace.

She looked up from the photos. "So the visions you saw were of Blackwell killing your brother, not you. Right?"

"It seems that way. But first, I want to do some online research to see if I can figure out if this is real or not," Scott said. "It could be a hoax, maybe from one of our test subjects."

"But the pictures…"

"They could have been altered," he said.

"And if it turns out to be true?"

"I don't know."

"She painted a very ugly picture of Dr. Blackwell," Grace said.

"He was a very ugly man."

***

Newspaper obituaries are deceptive. Sure, they reveal information about the deceased but that information is selective. Family members, friends, and clergy may suggest or even insist on those items that ultimately end up in the obituary. If a person died of certain illnesses, that may be left out. If their success was in an area that others might find offensive, that information might be excluded. Some information might be embellished. Scott had to carefully inspect the obituary to gather the correct information.

Research was easier than Scott thought it would be. He pulled key phrases out of the obituary, like, "Forty-three years old" and "Special Olympics, 1225 G Street," surrounded them with quotation marks and performed an internet search. A link to the original, un-redacted obituary appeared.

He discovered Kevin's last name was Martin. He had lived in Pennsylvania. A photograph on the original obituary looked identical to Scott, confirming he was a twin.

Two groups had been identified as recipients of gifts in Kevin's name. He contacted both, but neither would give out information. He contacted his wife, saying he knew Kevin in college, but she sensed something was wrong, said she had never heard of Scott Moore, and threatened to call the police. He assumed she thought he was some slimy ambulance chaser.

Ultimately, he came away with three confirmations: Scott had a twin brother, he was no longer living, and Dr. Blackwell killed him.

Scott felt somewhat relieved to know for sure Paul Blackwell was an evil man. It lessened the guilt Scott felt about not preventing his death.

This chapter of Scott's life seemed over but he

would enter the next with new knowledge of his unique ability.

He wondered how his life might be different.

CHAPTER ELEVEN

Scott returned to a half-assed effort of job hunting. The bottle of Alprazolam sat on the top shelf of his medicine cabinet.

One morning he received a call from his old college friend, Jeff Gray.

"Long time," Scott said. "What's up?"

"I'm sorry to bother you, but I thought I might ask for some of your Human Resources advice," Jeff said.

"Sure," Scott answered. "But can't you go to your own HR department?"

"Those idiots don't know anything about HR. Besides, I'd rather talk with you. I'll buy lunch."

Jeff seldom offered to buy anything and Scott felt this unique opportunity could not be missed. He agreed and met Jeff at a nice restaurant near Jeff's office. While dining on over-priced salads among other office workers, Jeff explained his situation. "It's this new kid, Chris," he began. "He's okay— very bright—but I get a bad feeling that he's not legit." Scott couldn't help but notice Jeff ate like a recently-freed starving man, shoveling lettuce, olives, croutons, and whatever else lined the salad bar into his mouth.

"What do you mean?"

"I don't know. I just believe he's an illegal alien."

"Didn't HR do a background check? Didn't he file the proper forms."

"Forms can be faked," Jeff said. "A talented kid could create a forgery with the software on a laptop."

"So what makes you think that he's an undocumented worker?"

"First, none of his family speaks English. You'd think they would have learned the language if they were here permanently."

"That's not necessarily true these days," Scott reacted.

"It's just a feeling I get. He never talks about long-term plans. He hangs that damn Mexican flag from the mirror of his car." Jeff threw his hands up in the air. "I just don't trust him."

"How's his work?" Scott asked.

"I can't argue with that. He's got some ideas about solar energy that have surprised some of our best engineers."

"If he's doing great work and his paperwork checks out, what do you care?"

"Solterra could get into serious trouble, right? They could be fined by the government. We might lose some grants."

"But you have nothing to go on—no reason to doubt his status."

"It's just a feeling—my gut." After a long pause, he added, "I don't trust him. I…uh, I think he's hitting on my wife."

"Has he done anything to make you believe that? Any evidence?"

"She talks a lot about him. And, whenever she's with us, he can't seem to take his eyes off her."

It was Scott's turn to pause. "Personally, I think you should trust Amy. She loves you." He stabbed a tomato. "But, if you really have doubts, go to your HR group and ask them to investigate him more completely. Talk with the advisor from Tech. Certainly both groups have vetted him thoroughly."

"Like I said, our HR is a bunch of bozos and I thought the people at Tech were losers back when you and I went to school there," Jeff said. "Do me a favor, first. Talk with the kid. Feel him out. Maybe he'll spill the beans to you."

Jeff seemed desperate. Scott wasn't sure why he agreed to do it, but he did. "All right. I'll talk to him. But paybacks are hell," he said. "Keep your eyes peeled in your HR department and let me know if anything opens up over there, okay?"

"You come to work in our HR department? You're so far above them, I don't think they'd consider you."

"Just let me know if anything opens up, okay?"

The two men agreed and Scott lined up a dinner with Chris Azorin at their house. He'd ask a few questions and see how Chris answered them. And maybe he'd pop a pill of Alprazolam and do a reading after Chris had gone home. He'd get to the bottom of this one way or the other.

***

Grace could barely contain her excitement when she heard Scott had invited Chris for dinner. "Fun! He seemed like a nice young man."

"Yeah. I thought we'd just check in and see how things were going."

"It's too cold to grill out," she said. "I'll cook a roast."

Scott was surprised. Now that he was no longer on a payroll, luxuries like roast dinners were rare. But he knew he couldn't change her mind. The plans were set.

***

Chris arrived a few minutes late, with flowers in one hand and a bottle of wine in the other. A cream-colored shirt embroidered with two columns of blue flowers hugged his muscled chest. He looked like he had bulked up. His black goatee had morphed into a tightly-trimmed beard. Grace met him at the door and he gave her a warm peck on the cheek.

Scott, who had just taken one of the Alprazolam pills, stepped forward. "Welcome," he said, extending his hand.

Chris shook it warmly and said, "Thank you for inviting me to dinner and thank you again for helping me get this job."

"That's what we do," Scott said. "Dinner, that is. You got the job on your own merits."

Grace's roast beef was tender and succulent. Chris raved about it throughout the meal. "You should taste my mother's *arroz con pollo*. It's not as good as this, but I'm sure you'd like it."

Pouring a third glass of wine, Scott asked how things were going at Solterra.

Chris swirled the wine around in his glass and said, "Amazing. We are tapping into some solar concepts that aren't even in the journals at school yet. I will surely include them in my doctoral thesis."

"Really?" Grace asked.

"Yes, ma'am. We've found a way to increase energy output, to amplify it, if you will, exponentially. This will drive down the cost of solar energy. It will reduce the need for fossil fuels and for our presence in the Middle East. No one in our industry can touch us."

"Sounds like Solterra is going to grow fairly rapidly," Scott said.

"If that happens," Chris said, "I will tell them they need to bring you onboard to manage all of the new employees."

He sensed a tinge of insincerity in Chris' words. "That would be nice."

"It would brighten up our company to have you and your beautiful wife attend our corporate parties," he said, winking at Grace.

Scott deemed the flirting harmless. It really didn't hurt for Grace to hear she was beautiful from someone other than Scott. Still, his charm set him off a bit. "Do you smoke cigars?" he asked Chris.

"Rarely."

"Well, this is a rare occasion. Let's step out onto the back porch and light up a stinker." Then in a lower voice, "Grace won't let me smoke inside."

Gumby followed the two men onto the back porch where they settled into comfortable chairs. Scott offered one to Chris and the two men lit up, inhaling the strong aroma. As soon as they exhaled, the poor dog's nose began running like a faucet and he started sneezing as if he'd snorted pepper. Scott tugged him back inside and closed the sliding glass door so he wouldn't bother them. "Better for him and for us," he said, returning to his chair. The dog pressed his wet nose against the flat glass, fogging it.

"Where do you see yourself in ten years, Chris?"

"Oh, I'd like to still be working at Solterra, maybe in an upper management position."

"That could happen. You don't want to go back to Mexico?"

"Oh, I'm not from Mexico," Chris said. "My parents came to the U.S. before I was born."

"That's right," Scott said, shaking his head. "I thought you'd come here for Tech."

"Oh, I like Mexico," Chris continued. "We still have relatives across the border and I go back to visit them every couple of years, but America is my home. I'm an American and I'll never move away."

"Never say never," Scott said. "Who knows. Solterra may ask you to head up their new solar farm there."

Chris chuckled, scrutinizing the smoldering tip of his cigar. "It could happen."

***

Chris left for home about 9:00 P.M. and Grace finished loading the dishwasher. Scott went into the living room to read Chris. He leaned back in the chair and relaxed until he could see Chris' images. The more he read people, the easier he found it to do. He could maneuver in and out of scenes, at will. He chose a scene to view.

He instantly recognized it. He had viewed it before. The day he had met Chris and had passed out at the gym, the images had come to him piecemeal, fuzzy, and confusing. Now, everything was crisp and clear.

Again, he heard the honking of a car horn outside. Back in the dirty little house watching a young man and a woman pack to the light of a streetlamp through a bedroom window, he heard the woman—his mother?—say something about his shoes. "Rápidamente. Poner los zapatos." Then he bounced along a dirt road in the back of a pickup truck while his parents talked excitedly about going to America.

As in the first time, his butt hurt from bouncing on the floor of the old pickup truck.

That all seemed pretty conclusive. It looked to Scott like Chris had not grown up in San Antonio as he had said, but slipped across the border as a young child.

Scott had found what he wanted, but some voyeuristic instinct inside urged him on. He slipped into one of the other images.

Squeals of pleasure filled his ears. Hers were punctuated with diamond earrings. She urged him on and everything he did only served to raise her desire. She lowered her head almost to his chest, letting her long, blonde hair fall over his face. He had to turn his head to the side to spit the stringy mass from his mouth. She jerked her head back up, flinging the hair back over her shoulders and groaned with ecstasy. Then, she reached back and slapped him across the cheek. "More. I want more!"

He obliged.

Scott moved out of that scene and by-passed the scene of the woman breast-feeding a baby in the hospital and slipped into a new, unfamiliar one.

Voices were whispering about love and heat and passion. "I've wanted you since I saw you at the picnic at your house," Scott heard Chris say. *"I can't keep myself from you." He saw Amy, Jeff's wife, lying on a large bed, sweat glistening between her naked breasts. Her lips were quivering and her eyes were locked onto Chris' eyes. "Yes," she moaned. "Oh, my God." She pulled him into her.*

Scott felt like he was peeping in on forbidden territory, so he moved from that scene and into another.

Hundreds of people applauded Chris. He stood on a stage flanked by huge logos for the Nobel Prize. Someone spoke from a podium, describing the radical new process Dr. Chris Azorin had championed. The process enabled solar cells to generate far greater energy than ever before, paving the way for people around the world to use clean energy. The spokesman described how Chris and the engineering staff of Solterra had begun an energy revolution that would change the world. Applause again rang through the excited crowd.

Impressed, Scott slipped into another scene. He felt compelled, as if driving by a traffic accident and not being able to remove his eyes from the wreck. He had to see…

He heard a familiar voice speaking softly. He also heard Chris' voice, telling the woman how attractive he found her. "I knew you were exquisite the first moment I saw you, at the picnic."

Scott thought he had re-entered the episode with Amy by mistake.

The woman said something about how she shouldn't be there and he realized it wasn't Amy's voice, but it was familiar. "Please stay," Chris said.

"But Scott needs me," he heard Grace say. "He lost his job a year ago. He needs me." Chris hugged her tightly, kissed her neck, and rubbed against her. He pressed her back against the wall and held her face in his hands. "Scott ignored you, searching for some dream that didn't exist. I would never do that to you. You deserve so much more—so very much

more." He kissed her on the lips, tasting her. "I would worship you, Grace."

Scott burst from the reading and lay exhausted in his chair. There may have been other scenes he had not read, but he could not go back. His hair dripped sweat. His fingers trembled and his heart pounded.

Grace was somewhere else in the house. He could hear her moving things about.

Gumby pranced into the room to where Scott sat and licked his hand, tugging him back to reality. He flipped his hand over and gently stroked the dog's head and Gumby responded by leaning into Scott's hand.

"Gumby" Scott said. "Let's go for a walk."

***

Frustrated, shaking, scared, he took the dog for a marathon walk. Scott had to clear his head. Gumby was crazy-happy, with night smells and sounds to keep him busy. Scott, on the other hand, was disturbed beyond control. With no one else to talk to, he attempted to carry on a conversation with the happy-go-lucky hound on the end of his leash.

"So, Gumby. What do we know? We know Chris is a brilliant kid. He has potential. He can change our world for the better."

The dog huffed and puffed down the sidewalk, dragging Scott with him.

"I'm glad we agree on that. Also, we know that Chris can't keep his dick in his pants. The whole fucking world would be a better place if he'd just find a live-in girlfriend or two to keep him occupied and away from other men's wives."

Gumby stopped and plunged his nose into a bush.

"You can't understand," Scott explained. "After all, we had you neutered."

The two resumed their march through the neighborhood. Gumby tugged persistently on his leash.

"We also know, at least we're pretty sure, that he came to our country illegally. His birth certificate or documentation or whatever paperwork he used to get his job at Solterra must be forged. He's lied to his employer, to Jeff and to me."

They turned the corner and all but ran into a man walking a bulldog. Both dogs bared fangs and barked fiercely. Scott jerked back on the leash and physically dragged his dog into the street to avoid the squat, bow-legged beast. "Sorry!" he yelled back as they continued to walk through the neighborhood. The old man snorted. So did his dog.

"We also know that he may try to bed both Grace and Amy. Sometimes the visions don't come true, that's right. But the images imply that it could happen. Oh, hell. For that matter, anyone might try to go to bed with Grace. But the visions just make it that more plausible."

Gumby looked back at his master as if to say, "Make up your mind."

"So, what should I do?" Scott said aloud. "If I turn him in as an illegal alien, all my problems are solved. He never hits on Grace. I never have to kick his ass." Then he mumbled, "As if I could."

149

A cold breeze swept around a stand of pine trees and made him wrap his parka around himself tighter.

"But, then Solterra may fail to have its breakthrough technology and the world may struggle along without the new technology. Sure, somebody would probably eventually develop the same thing, but that could be five, ten, twenty years down the road. From that perspective, it's a no-brainer. Keep quiet about his citizenship and keep him away from Grace."

Seduced by a scent, Gumby pulled Scott across the road toward a side-street. "I could tell Grace about the vision. I probably should, but she might think I'm just being insecure. And, I might plant ideas in her head. What am I saying? She would never allow herself to go to bed with that young, Hispanic stud."

"Gumby, it's time to go home."

***

The clouds opened up like a massive door to a sanctuary and a light drizzle soaked Scott and his boxer as they made their way back to the house. Gumby didn't hesitate to display his intense dislike for the cold rain by laying his ears flat against his head and shaking off the wetness every ten steps or so.

Scott pushed the pair into a jog two blocks from home, but came to a dead stop in front of the house. Chris' Ford truck was parked in his driveway.

Scott stared into the kitchen window to see

Grace and Chris laughing. She patted his shoulder as she giggled. They were both standing just inches apart, much too close for Scott.

He had seen enough. He deliberately barged through the back door into the kitchen.

Grace and Chris jumped apart as if shocked by a bolt of electricity.

"Hi, honey," Grace managed.

"Mr. Moore," Chris said. "I left my jacket." He could not have sounded more defensive if he had tried.

"Yes," Grace added. "He came back for his jacket."

Scott looked toward the closet where he had hung Chris' jacket several hours before. It was still hanging on the coat hanger.

Gumby shook again, spraying rain droplets over everyone in the kitchen.

"Scott. Why did you bring the dog in the house when he's so wet?" Grace pulled a dish towel from a drawer and tossed it to Scott and then grabbed one for Chris, who had been christened by Gumby. Scott dragged Gumby to the porch, then marched to the closet and pulled Chris' jacket from the hanger. "Here's your jacket," he said. "Don't want you to forget it again."

Chris took the jacket from Scott and handed the towel back to Grace. "Uhm, thank you."

The two men squared off for a moment as if they might fight. Then Chris averted his gaze and shrugged the jacket on. "Thanks again for a wonderful dinner," he said and walked out of the house.

Grace stood stock still. "What are you doing?" she shouted.

"What am I doing?"

"Yes."

"The question is, what are you doing?"

"We were just talking," Grace said. "That is all."

"It looked pretty cozy from the street."

"Nothing happened," Grace said, emphatically. "Do you think I would be so stupid as to have a silly fling while you were out walking the dog? If I wanted to bone Chris, I could have done it anytime you were at Blackwell's office. After all, you've spent a lot of time there over the last few weeks."

"Well, you don't have that option anymore, do you?"

"I guess I'll have to be more creative."

"Look, Grace. I read him. I saw Chris having an affair with Amy." He didn't mention the incident he'd read between Chris and Grace. "If he's willing to cheat on his boss' wife, he wouldn't hesitate to cheat with my wife, too."

"Scott, it takes two to cheat. Do you think that lowly of me?" The glare in her eyes portrayed betrayal, not guilt.

Scott's cheeks burned. He dropped his head. "I'm sorry, Grace. I...I don't know what to say."

Grace stared at him, wrinkles crowding her forehead. "When you figure it out, let me know." She stormed out of the kitchen.

"I just don't trust that kid," Scott shouted after her. But he couldn't say why.

CHAPTER TWELVE

Scott slept on the sofa again that night. When he woke up, Grace had already left for the airport. She and several other nurses from the hospital travelled together to a convention in Orlando. A note beside the sofa said,

I do love you, Scott. I'll be back in three days.

He shaved and showered and deliberated on his next steps. Through the night he had wrestled with his lumpy sofa almost as much as he did with his anger and his guilt over their fight. And in the middle of it all was the incredible potential that Chris Azorin just might have working for Solterra. He was one of the only people alive who just might make a real impact on the world.

In the morning solitude Scott resolved to give the kid, the philandering, adulterous kid, a shot and then get the hell out. He and Grace would move far away. She could find a job in another hospital in another city and he could hunt for a new HR position with another company.

But still he wondered. He had to know if Chris could really pull it off.

Maybe Jeff held the key.

He arrived at the Solterra office at about 8:30 A.M., asked the security guard to call Jeff Gray's office, and took a seat in the expansive lobby. Photographs of various green energy projects ordained the walls. A brass tag on each piece of furniture indicated it had been constructed using the finest in recycled technology. A rather large plate on the wall proclaimed the carpet in the building was also made of recycled fibers. Another tag proclaimed the light bulbs in the lobby were from reclaimed materials. Solterra was definitely green.

Within a few minutes, the guard called Scott over, gave him a visitor's badge, and instructed him to take the elevator to the eighteenth floor. He stopped at a water fountain beside the elevator and washed down one of the Alprazolam tablets and punched the up button. The elevator looked out of place in its normalcy. No recycled tags or green energy project announcement. Just a row of buttons, a floor LED display, and the ubiquitous elevator inspection notice.

Jeff met Scott when the elevator doors opened with an enthusiastic handshake and a slap on the back. He escorted Scott down a hall lined with more photographs of Solterra projects, to his corner office.

Scott knew Jeff's office would be nicer than any he'd ever had. Engineers always had nicer digs than

HR. Everyone always had nicer digs than HR. Jeff's was a corner office. Large full-length glass windows lined two walls. A flat screen monitor occupied most of the third. Jeff even had a small sofa and a couple of chairs beneath the monitor. Behind his desk, various awards and trophies acknowledged the accomplishments of the office's occupant.

"Cappuccino? Latte?" Jeff asked as he pulled Scott into the office and motioned for him to sit on the sofa.

Scott shook his head, although he would have liked a coffee. He just didn't want to stay there long enough for the coffee to arrive. Jeff was a self-centered bore. Just get in, make the connection, get the vision, and get out.

"I like your office," Scott said politely.

"Ah, it's okay. I'd really rather be up on the C-level but the building's only got so many spaces. Maybe next year. These yahoos just don't know how to treat talent, you know?"

Scott nodded, but he really didn't know. As one of those talent-treating yahoos in other companies, he thought they'd treated their talent quite well, and from the look of Jeff's office, he didn't seem to be in the slightest mistreated.

"So did you get to talk to our boy?"

"Yeah. Grace and I had him over for dinner last night. Had a great time."

"And...?"

"I think you've got yourself a superstar there, Jeff-o. I'm not an expert on solar energy, but Chris seems to have his shit very well put together. He's a keeper," Scott lied, not wanting to stir Jeff's lack of trust.

"Did you get a sense for his background? Did he say if he was legal?"

"He says he was born in El Paso," Scott said. "I have no reason to doubt his word," he lied. He felt his palms begin to sweat. "I have no reason to believe he didn't grow up in San Antonio."

"You think he's a legitimate citizen?"

"I haven't seen his birth certificate, but I'd figure he's as legitimate as any of us." Scott paused for a moment to see if Jeff was buying it and then continued the sales job. "If he's an undocumented worker, tell him to bring back fifty more of his friends. We need illegals just like him."

"I don't know. I just don't trust him."

"Hell, Jeff. You don't trust anybody."

Jeff stared at Scott for a long moment and Scott thought he might have said the wrong thing. Then Jeff burst out laughing. "I guess you're right. And that's how I got where I am today."

"Let me tell you," Scott continued. "This kid loves it here at Solterra. He says you guys are about to turn the industry on its ear."

"He didn't divulge any secrets, did he?"

Scott knew more about Chris than Chris knew about himself, but he wasn't about to let Jeff know that. "Like I would understand what he said if he did?"

"Yeah, right," Jeff said not realizing how condescending he was.

"When you guys go public, let me know," Scott said. "I wanna get in on that IPO."

"Yeah, you and everyone else."

"If I were you, I'd take this new kid you've got and give him free rein—ride him for all he's worth. He'll pay you back many times over." Scott didn't say anything about how tight Jeff needed to hold the reins on his wife.

Jeff stood and Scott followed. "I'll walk down to the 'levitator with you," he said and Scott knew that was his best over-used line.

When the doors opened, Jeff said, "Well, I thank you for your valued opinion. If I can ever repay the favor, let me know."

"Well, I'm glad you asked. If you know of any companies like Solterra, you know, maybe in another city, that might be searching for an HR guy…"

Jeff chuckled. "You never give up, do you?" He extended his hand.

The elevator stopped on the sixth floor and Chris Azorin stepped through the doors. A scent of sautéed onions and peppers, clouded with heavy cologne, lingered. Instantly the atmosphere became charged and chilled. It took every ounce of Scott's will to keep him from decking the kid right there and demanding he stay away from Grace. "Hi, Chris," he said in as pleasant a voice as he could. Scott felt like he could cut the icy atmosphere with a chain saw. He made a conscious effort to avoid touching Chris, since he didn't want his visions to mix with those from Jeff.

"Mr. Moore," Chris said. "What brings you to Solterra?"

"I just wanted to talk with my old friend, Jeff

157

Gray," Scott said.

"Oh, what about?"

"This and that."

He knew Chris would worry about his conversation with Jeff and Scott was happy to let him sweat it out. "Take care," he called when the elevator arrived in the lobby. Scott handed the guard his visitor's pass and signed out.

He was sweating like a convict on death row.

***

His hands were shaking when he climbed in his Prius in the parking lot of Solterra. He had not planned on bumping into Chris Azorin and the encounter unnerved him.

Leaning back in his seat, he forced himself to relax. He allowed the pill he had taken earlier to take effect and opened himself to the visions of Jeff he saw. He honed in on Jeff Gray's stories like a searchlight. He had to see what might transpire between Jeff and Chris, especially since Chris had the potential to be a real worldwide game changer.

He saw image after image of relatively mundane events, science fairs, merit badge awards, weddings, and promotions. Jeff had a lot of them. Then, he stumbled upon one that was unmistakably relevant.

Jeff drove by his white two-story house at the end of the cul-de-sac in a neighborhood of glamorous homes owned by wealthy people. He turned around and headed away from the house.

Chris' truck was parked a block up the street. He

passed it, and headed down the road a ways.

Parking in front of Taylor's Gun Shop on Main Street, he stepped down from his Suburban. A look at his watch confirmed that it was past ten o'clock, so the store should be open. Handguns, rifles, and ammunition lined the walls all around the shop. He approached the glass case on the right and worked his way left until he found a simple, straightforward pistol. He asked the store salesman if he could see the gun and held the revolver with a rubber grip in his hand, feeling its weight. Scott heard him say, "I'll take this one and some shells."

Scott worked frantically to see the image of the credit card receipt that Jeff signed. He couldn't make out the date. He cursed under his breath when he saw Jeff hand it over to the salesman. He still could not see the date.

The scene changed. Jeff was stopped down the street from his house.

Jeff pushed six rounds into the gun. He opened the car door and marched straight down the middle of the street toward his house. Looking down, he saw the gun in his right hand, pointed toward the road.

He extracted the house keys from his pocket and unlocked the front door. Quietly, he closed the door behind him and walked back toward the master bedroom. Noises of passion echoed from behind the bedroom door. He saw Jeff's hand reach for the door knob.

He shoved the door open. Amy was on her back,

legs drawn up high. Chris was on top between her legs. Jeff raised the gun and pulled the trigger once. Blood splattered out of Chris' naked back. He fired again. Chris' head shot forward and bone mass, brain, and hair splattered over the headboard. He fired a third time and Amy jolted in bed. Her breast splattered into a fleshy pulp. Jeff fired a fourth time and Amy's face was blown away.

Scott was shouting, uncontrollably, "Oh, my God! Don't do it. No!"

He watched as Jeff pulled the gun up to the side of his head and pulled the trigger.

Scott bolted out of his car, shouting, "No. Jeff, don't do it." His vision had not returned fully and he ran full force into the side of a panel van. He bounced off the van and staggered toward the entrance to Solterra. Employees ran toward Scott to offer their help.

"I've gotta stop Jeff Gray," Scott yelled. "He's got a gun. He's gonna kill them."

Someone screamed. Security guards appeared from around the corner and raced toward him. Someone else yelled something about a gun. A security guard yelled at him to stop.

"We've got to stop Jeff," he said to the guard. "He will kill them."

The guard pulled a Taser and moments later Scott felt as if someone had plugged him into a bolt of lightning. Every muscle in his body seemed to tighten up at once. He could feel the electricity pulsing through him from the tiny harpoons stuck in his stomach. He fell to the smooth granite floor, banging his head hard.

Finally, he blacked out.

***

He felt like he'd been punched in the gut with a hammer. The two puncture wounds in his stomach made by the Taser were oozing some rank moisture and they itched like hell. His head ached and he had a lump the size of a walnut on the back of his skull. All of this was complicated by an overwhelming smell of urine somewhere nearby.

With difficulty he raised his head and looked around. He was in jail. No one else occupied this particular cell, although he could hear voices echoing from nearby cells. The Solterra security guards had called the police who placed Scott in the backseat of a patrol car and escorted him to the local police station. He had tried to call Grace from the station, but her cell phone was off or out of cell tower range or on vibrate or stuffed in the bottom of her purse. "Grace," Scott almost shouted when her voicemail message came on. "I need help. I had another vision—panicked in the parking lot of Solterra while trying to warn Jeff. I'm so sorry. We'll talk later. But the security guards tased me and the police have arrested me. I need you to bail me out of jail. I'm sorry."

He tried to pull himself up into a sitting position, but his stomach was too sore. He rolled to his side until his hips were almost off the little bed on which he lay. From there he pushed his body up with his right hand and swung his legs down to reach a sitting position. He leaned forward and supported his aching head in his hands with arms propped on his knees. He felt he was going to vomit. Forcing himself to breathe in deeply, he instinctively sensed his brain needed blood to counteract the dizzy feeling. Within a few moments, he was feeling a bit more stable.

"Well, you are alive," he heard a voice say. "How you feelin'?"

"Like shit."

"That's what most people say in here," he said.

"Is that supposed to be comforting?"

"Just being straight. I'm trying to break the ice."

"It ain't working," Scott said. "Who are you anyway?" He looked up and saw a younger man wearing a corduroy jacket and jeans standing outside his cell.

"My name's Gordon Thompson," the man said. He held a thick book of some sort across his chest like a shield.

"And how will breaking the ice with Gordon Thompson help me?" Scott asked.

"I'll be straight with you," he said. "I'm here to tell you that God loves you and wants to help you in this tough time."

Scott groaned and laid his head back against the concrete block wall. The lump on his skull burned with pain.

"You've probably gone through life without knowing that Jesus wants to be your friend," Gordon said. He had an odd accent and the word came out as, "free-ind." "A life of sin is no life at all. Romans 3:23 says, 'For all have sinned and fallen short of the glory of God.' Most of us don't think we need God. Most of us think we can do it all on our own. But most of us arwrong."

Scott let the man drone on and on.

And he did. "John 3:16 says, 'For God so loved the world that He gave His only begotten son that whosoever believeth in him might not die but have eternal life.' Jesus loves you, my friend, no matter what you've done. He knows your heart. He knows about your sins. Yet, He still loves you, even you, uh, what did you say your name was?"

"Gordo," Scott said slowly. "You don't know a thing about me. Not what I've done. Not who I am. Not even my name."

Gordon's left hand gripped one of the steel bars between them like he was hanging on for his life. He seemed surprised by Scott's reaction.

Scott stretched through the bars and latched onto Gordon's hand. "You don't know that I became a Christian at the age of thirteen at summer camp. You don't know that I'm in here because of a huge misunderstanding."

"That's what everybody says." He yanked his hand away.

"You don't know if I'm a saint or a sinner. You don't know if I'm not Satan himself," Scott said and leered at the young man. "Until you take the time to get to know me, don't you dare waste my time by trying to tell me what you think I ought to do to straighten out my life. Is that straight enough for you?"

"Uh, yes sir," Gordon said. He turned to go and then, as an afterthought called back, "I'll be praying for you."

"I sincerely hope so," Scott said.

He leaned back against the wall, carefully. Too much movement, too fast, would upset what little equilibrium he felt there was left in the world and chaos would ensue.

He wondered if the Alprazolam might still be effective, so he allowed himself to relax. Instantly, he saw several images. He chose the nearest one and found he was watching one of Gordon's visions. Scott wasn't surprised by what he saw.

"Gordo!" he yelled down the hall.

"Yes, my friend?" Gordon called back. He hadn't left, yet. "Did you want to talk?"

"Naah," Scott called. "Just thought you might want to stop watching that porn on your laptop. Your wife's gonna catch you and, boy does she have a temper."

When the cat-calls from the other inmates quieted down, Scott listened for Gordon's reply. But it never came.

All he heard was the slamming of the exit door.

***

A couple of hours later, a guard came by Scott's cell. Scott was awake and trying to determine his next steps, but wasn't coming to any conclusions.

"You were pretty tough on your visitor," the guard said. "He was just trying, in his own way, to help out."

Scott looked up from the bed where he had been sitting since he woke up. His head ached. His back was sore. The wounds in his stomach still hurt and he was exhausted. "Yeah. You're right. It's been a tough day. I guess I took it out on him," he said.

The guard went on, "I heard about your day. You caused quite a stir over at Solterra. They said you were running around the parking lot saying you had a gun and somebody was going to be killed."

Scott groaned. "I don't have a gun. I wasn't going to hurt anyone."

"Well, you scared a lot of people over there."

Scott had been pretty scared, himself.

"You'll be happy to know that we heard from your wife. She was out of town at a conference."

"Yeah, she's in Orlando."

"Not anymore. She's on her way back. When she gets here she'll post bail."

"Ohhh," Scott moaned.

"Most people are happy to hear someone is coming to post bail. It almost sounds like you like it here."

"Believe me, Mister. I'm not most people." He leaned back against the concrete blocks of the cell wall. Echoes of voices from other cells bounced around his and into his head. He closed his eyes but could not rest. Exhausted, he began to fear the voices were the beginning of another reading—that he was reliving someone's vision over and over and could not stop. If he couldn't control the visions, he would go insane.

He lay back down and dozed in an out of consciousness for the next couple of hours.

"Scott Moore," the guard called. "Moore. Your bail has been posted."

He rolled over and pushed himself into a sitting position again. Gradually, slowly so as not to disturb the delicate balance of the world around him, he stood up. The cell began to spin and he held onto the wall for support. He staggered through the open cell door, taking each step carefully. The guard escorted him past other cells filled with inmates who made cat-calls, obscene gestures, and pleas for help as he stumbled by.

Grace looked so out of place in the station lobby. When the officer opened the door and she saw Scott, she ran to hug him. "Oh, Scotty. What happened? Are you all right?"

"Can we go?" Scott begged.

Grace checked with the sergeant on duty and then helped her husband out the front doors of the police station.

"What is going on?" Grace asked after they both had fastened seat belts.

"Grace, I read Jeff this morning. I had to see how he fit into what I read from Chris last night. I told you I saw Chris and Amy."

"So?"

"The vision was so clear, so real, it freaked me out." He looked about Grace's car, searching for the right words to say. "I saw Jeff drive by his house and spot Chris' truck. Then he went to Taylor's Gun Shop and bought a pistol. It had to be current day. The cars were modern," Scott continued to search for the right words. "Then, I saw him walking down the middle of his street with a pistol in his hand. He entered his house, went back to his bedroom, and blew two holes each in Chris and Amy while they

166

made love in his bed."

Scott was aware of how strange and melodramatic his descriptions sounded. He felt helpless to describe what he had experienced accurately. "Finally, he put the gun to his head and pulled the trigger."

"Oh, dear," was all Grace could mutter.

"After I saw that, I panicked. I ran into the parking lot and tried to find Jeff to warn him. The security guards thought I was threatening to hurt him so they tased me."

He stared into Grace's eyes. She searched his, trying to discern every ounce of truth. Finally, she reached down to his stomach, "Did it hurt?"

"Like hell," he said. "Every muscle in my body contracted. I was in serious pain."

"Well I need to get you home and do my job as your nurse," she said.

And she did. She put an antiseptic on the Taser wounds and covered them with tape and gauze. Then she took him to bed.

That night, with Gumby sleeping fitfully at the foot of the bed, she rocked Scott to sleep. "I don't know if this ability is a gift or a curse," she whispered to him just before he drifted off. "A gift or a curse."

***

Early the next morning, Scott woke with thoughts of Jeff Gray crowding his mind. He had to somehow warn him about Chris. Yet he couldn't let on as to how he knew Chris might be a threat.

After a shave and a shower, he hustled into the kitchen for a relatively quick breakfast of Cheerios, while he watched the clock, waiting for the time Jeff should arrive at work. When it reached eight twenty-five, he picked up the phone and dialed Solterra.

"I'd like to speak to Jeff Gray, please," Scott said after the receptionist answered the call.

"One moment, please."

Scott waited. He tapped his toe. He flicked his ink pen cap over and over. Finally, the receptionist came back on the line.

"I'm sorry. Jeff isn't taking your call," she said.

"Why not?" He damned Caller I.D. beneath his breath.

"I don't know that."

Scott hung up and turned on his laptop computer. He typed out a quick email to Jeff asking him to call as soon as he could. Within minutes it bounced back with the message that it had been blocked by the Solterra address.

He thought of calling Chris at home. He might not be in the office, yet. But what would he say? "Chris, stay away from Jeff's wife." That sounded stupid and he felt it wouldn't work. Besides, the vision he had may not come true for weeks or even months. Regardless, nothing he could do would stop Chris.

Grace was still in bed, so Scott dressed quietly and slipped out the back door. He drove his Prius to the Solterra offices.

Feeling cautious and a bit frightened and embarrassed because of his reaction to the vision the day before, Scott slowly walked up the steps to the Solterra offices.

A security guard met him at the door. "I'm sorry, Mr. Moore, but you are not allowed in the Solterra offices," he said.

"Why not? I was just here yesterday."

"You also frightened a number of employees yesterday, so you have been banned from the premises." He crossed arms over his chest.

"I need to speak to Jeff Gray," Scott said. "Will you ask him to meet me in the parking lot?"

"We will file an injunction, if necessary, to restrict you from coming on our property," the guard answered.

"Can you ask him to meet me off-site?"

The guard didn't say anything. He just stared at Scott.

Frustrated and angry, Scott returned to his car. He grabbed a pen and paper and jotted a quick note on a pad of paper.

Jeff, I'm concerned about your relationship with Chris Azorin. Please don't do anything rash.

He read over the note several times. It was vague enough so as not to encourage him to suspect his wife and Chris might have an affair, yet he couldn't tell if it was specific enough to prevent Jeff from doing anything foolish, like buy a gun and kill them.

He folded the note and drove around the lot until

he spied Jeff's Suburban. He climbed out of the car and tucked the note under the windshield wiper of Jeff's vehicle.

He drove off feeling far from finished, but he didn't know what else he could do.

"Where have you been?" Grace asked when he entered their house.

"I had to see Jeff. I had to tell him about the vision I had with he and Chris and Amy."

"What did he say?"

"He refused to meet with me."

"Did you try calling?"

"I phoned him, emailed him, and finally left a note on his car."

"I guess there's nothing else you can do."

"I just feel so helpless. What good is it to see people's futures if they won't let you help them?"

"Perhaps we should back off this vision stuff," Grace said. "It doesn't seem to be doing anyone any good, least of all, you."

Scott listened, feeling helpless. He felt as if he would suffocate. There was nothing, absolutely nothing he could do.

CHAPTER THIRTEEN

Grace drove. She rolled the back windows half-way down because Gumby sat there. The morning air blew away their cares as the miles swept by and Scott wondered why they didn't take long road trips more often. It was a fluke that they were taking this one. Just a few hours earlier, they had been stuck in their house pondering what to do next.

Grace's boss, a battle-ax who followed hospital policies as if they were written by God Himself and handed down on stone tablets, had insisted she take some time off. "Get away. Take Scott and sit on a hill somewhere and think about nothing but each other."

"I don't have any vacation days left."

"Sure you do. I've got this report—oh, where was that—I just laid it on the desk. Anyway, I'm positive you've got two weeks coming to you. By the time you get back, I'll have it straightened out."

"Go to the beach," one of her friends urged. "Wriggle your toes in the sand and wade in the water."

171

"It's October," Grace reminded her. "I'm not wading in any water 'til next June."

"Go to New York," another nurse suggested. "Catch a couple of shows. Visit some museums."

"Too noisy," Grace said and the Big Apple would wait. "We need to go someplace to relax and rest. We need a place where we can just sit and think and talk."

"How 'bout a staycation? Don't go anywhere but here."

"No, we need a place that is inspiring." She pondered the dilemma. "Maybe we could rent a house." She spent an hour searching the internet for vacation rentals without luck.

Scott walked in with a turkey sandwich and a glass of tea—an offering if repentance—and placed them on the desk before her.

"I forgot the leaves change this time of year in the mountains," she said. "Every house, cabin, trailer, or lean-to I've checked is booked."

"What about that one?" Scott asked, pointing to a listing featuring mountain views and everlasting memories. "Sounds perfect."

"The posting says it's booked. But...they may know of something else." She dialed the number.

"Hello?"

"Hi. I saw your listing for a cabin in the mountains online. My husband and I are looking for a place to rent immediately."

"Hmmm. I've got two cabins, but both are rented. You know, this time of year, things fill up fast."

"I know. This opportunity just came up. Do you

know of any other rentals in the area that might be available?"

"How long do you want to stay?"

"A week. Maybe two."

"Well, I may have something for you. It's a bit unusual."

Grace shot a hopeful smile up at Scott who was taking a bite out of her turkey sandwich.

"I've got this place up here behind me that's not ready yet for renters. I had hoped to have it fixed up by now, but just didn't get it done."

"Is it rustic?" Grace asked with hesitation in her voice.

"Oh, no," he said. "Just needs a little paint and a little caulk. I'll make you a deal. If you and your husband will spend a couple of hours each day painting the interior and caulking the windows, I'll let you have it for free. I'll email you some photos," he added.

The pictures were gorgeous. The little two bedroom cabin looked perfect as it was. Grace called back and set the reservation. They packed and left.

***

Brilliant bright red leaves lined the highway as they wove their way through the mountains. Gumby hung his head out the rear window and lapped up every mountain scent and taste he could. Scott quietly waited in the passenger seat feeling somewhat like the little boy being sent to detention and somewhat like a kid going on a family

173

vacation—same thing.

They passed several small mountain towns on the way to Waynesville. Just outside the city, they turned onto a two-lane road and then again to a one-lane road that took them up the mountain on a steep ascent that slowed the Prius and popped their ears. Halfway up the mountain the road began to swerve with a series of S-turns and zig-zags above narrow ravines that dropped hundreds of feet. "I'd hate to take this road after a snowfall," Scott said, leaning this way and that. Gumby braced himself in the back, feet firmly planted, and toenails digging into the thin carpet as much as possible. Once they had to pull way over into a ditch to allow an oversized pickup truck room to pass.

They pulled off onto another side road and came to a stop on a ridge overlooking waves and waves of mountains peppered by housetops. "This will do nicely," Grace said. Below them on one side a white clapboard house nestled into the landscape overlooking the scenic view. On the other side, wooden steps and a rustic railing ascended the mountain to a smaller cabin.

Grace turned the engine off and stepped outside breathing in the cool mountain air. "This is incredible," she called to Scott who was attempting to exit the car and keep Gumby from doing so at the same time.

"Hello," called a broad-shouldered man as he stepped from the porch of the larger house. "I'm Tom," he said. His high forehead betrayed his age, but still, he seemed fairly spry for an older guy. "Tom Jackson," he added.

174

"Grace Moore," she said. "This is my husband, Scott."

The trio shook hands and Tom took them and the rambunctious mutt for a tour. The cabin was perfect. Tom was obviously remodeling it and almost all of his work had been done. Signs of expert craftsmanship were evident throughout the house.

"Do you do all of the work yourself?" Scott asked.

"Just about."

"You obviously have some woodworking skill."

"Thanks. I just keep at it. I guess it helps me stay out of trouble," he said with a gleam in his eye.

It turned out only two of the bedrooms needed paint and three or four of the windows lacked fresh caulk. Scott and Grace knew they were getting the deal of a lifetime. They offered to pay for their stay.

"I can't do it," Tom said. "We had an agreement. I honor my agreements."

They returned to the car and transported all of the luggage to the cabin. Tom wished them well and Scott and Grace set about settling in. She placed folded shirts in a dresser while he hung up some clothes in the closet. He paused and leaned against the doorjamb, watching his wife. Moved, stirred, he tip-toed over to her and embraced her from behind. Dragging backwards, he pulled her onto the cedar log-framed bed and the two bounced on the mattress in laughter.

After a moment, he pulled her over so she faced him. "Thank you, Grace," he said.

She kissed him warmly.

Scott was reminded of why he married her and confused as to why she stayed with him.

***

That afternoon, Scott rocked in a creaky, wooden rocking chair on the back porch, Gumby by his side, watching the layers of mountains shift and shuffle as the clouds came and went in front of the bright sun. He paused when he heard a voice, "Y'all home?"

Gumby first raised a head and then jumped up to all fours to discover who had come to visit. Scott rose to his feet, too, and greeted Tom Jackson striding up the steps behind the house.

"Nice view, isn't it?" Tom asked. "Mind if I join you?"

"My house is your house, literally," Scott said motioning to one of the chairs. As he had hoped, the mountain air and view had him feeling refreshed

Tom rolled back into the chair and started it rocking. The chair complained and the floor beneath it groaned. After several minutes of rocking the creaking chair back and forth, he asked, "Scott, what do you do back home?"

Scott answered, "I'm in Human Resources, at least I was until I was recently laid off. Grace is a nurse."

"HR? That's a noble profession," Tom said. "It usually doesn't get much respect from others, I'm afraid."

"You've got experience in corporate life?" Scott asked.

176

"Corporate life; an oxymoron. No. I know very little about corporations. But I think I have a handle on people and they work in corporations."

"True."

"And that's your focus, isn't it? People."

"Over twenty years," Scott said.

"That's a long time," he said, staring after the mountain range. He drew an aged hand to his chin and stroked it as if stroking a beard.

"Have you always been in the rental business?" Scott asked in an effort to be polite.

"No," Tom said. "This is my retirement hobby. Before retirement I was a Methodist minister. I still dabble in it a bit here and there. Preach some Sundays at a little church over in Upper Crabtree. Do some weddings now and then."

"Oh," Scott said. He had not had a one-on-one conversation with a minister since he was a kid in Catechism, except for that brief encounter with Rev. Gordon Thompson while he was in jail. He wasn't sure how to respond.

"But I hope you won't hold that against me," Tom said looking his way with that special gleam in his eye.

Scott shook his head.

Tom shot him a quick wink.

Scott felt his neck grow warm.

"Gotcha," Tom said.

"Yeah."

***

Grace came into the bedroom early the next

morning and gently shook Scott awake. He brushed her off. The fresh air made sleeping in late easy and he wanted to enjoy this treasure.

"Scott, I need to talk to you," she said softly.

"Later."

"Okay."

But he couldn't go back to sleep. The urgency in her voice, the level of concern kept him from staying in bed.

She was at the kitchen table when he shuffled out of the bedroom. "What's up?"

"Sit down, honey," she said, pulling out the chair next to her. She opened the laptop computer and turned it to face Scott. "You did everything you could. You tried to stop it."

The headline from their hometown paper said, "Man Kills Two, Then Self."

Scott didn't need to read more than the headline. "When did it happen?"

"Yesterday," Grace said. "It was just as in your vision."

Scott stared at the table. He had failed again. He saw it. He knew it would happen, but just not when. And he couldn't stop it.

"You did everything you could," Grace said again. She reached out and held Scott's hand.

Scott slowly pulled his hand away and stepped out on the back porch. Jeff was dead. Scott would never hear his sarcastic voice again. He had bought a handgun in a gun shop, taken it home, and killed Amy and her lover. Chris was dead. The world would continue to struggle without his genius and without his innovative ideas. What had the old lady said after Dr. Blackwell died? "What a waste."

Scott felt utterly helpless. "Why have an ability if you can't do anything with it?" he asked no one in particular. Tears filled his eyes blocking his view of the mountains.

Grace came out a moment later and wrapped her arms around his shoulders from behind. They stayed that way for a long time.

Scott couldn't see the mountains through his tears, but he heard the birds chirping nearby. He heard something rustle in the leaves down below and smelled smoke from nearby chimneys. It brought him back, reminding him that he was still here, away from home, but very much alive and kicking. Unlike Chris and Amy and Jeff.

He turned around and embraced Grace, holding her tight. "Such a waste," he said.

CHAPTER
FOURTEEN

It didn't take long for Scott to recall painting always brings out the best and worst in people. For those with any talent, any patience, any understanding of beauty, a little paint on a wall is a good thing. But Scott didn't have any of those attributes. He took the rag from his back pocket and wiped more drops of paint from the floor where they had fallen when he filled the pan with globs of white.

"Have I ever told you how much I hate painting?" he shouted to Grace who stroked a perfect thin line between the wall and the ceiling like a pro.

"No," she called back. "Not that I recall."

He rolled a thick, bubbly mass of paint against the wallboard and watched as a tiny river of white traced the bottom of the roller handle, flowed over his hand and down his arm to his elbow, where it dripped to the floor. "Son-of-a-Bitch," he jumped back, slinging more paint around the room. The mess bothered him a lot; a lot more than it should have. "I'm a total fuck-up!" he shouted.

"Whoa, Mister," Grace said, laying her brush down on a paint can lid and rushing into Scott's room. "I'm married to that man you're talking about there."

"Well you married a total fuck-up."

"I don't think so."

"I'm messing up this nice old guy's house, wasting his paint and he was so kind to let us use it this week."

"We can clean up any mess you make," she said.

"You always do that," he answered. "You clean up the messes I make. I get thrown in jail and you have to leave your conference to bail me out. I lose my job and you have to increase your shifts to make up the difference." His voice grew louder and higher in pitch. His throat began to constrict and his eyes began to water.

Gumby hated crying and shouting. He slinked into the kitchen to hide under the table.

"I can see the fucking future and I even fuck that up. I can't stop people from killing themselves even though I knew it was going to happen." He was ranting now, between sobs.

"That wasn't your fault," Grace said, trying to stop him, hold him. But he kept walking away from her.

"I'm given a detailed script of what will happen and I can't prevent it."

"Scott, Scott," Grace urged.

"Four people died, I knew they would, and I

couldn't save one of them," he cried.

She hugged him tightly. Scott felt his knees buckling from the stress and from his weakness. He dropped down and then rolled on his side and against Grace, who had lowered herself with him to catch him.

He felt her arms warmly around his head as she rocked him back and forth. "I saw Chris with you," he said through the sobs.

"I know you did. Through the kitchen window. We talked about that."

"No, I had a vision of Chris and he was making love to you," Scott said without looking at her face.

"That's preposterous," Grace said.

"It was as real as all of the other visions," he said.

"But some of them didn't come true," she said. "Neither did that one."

"Well, it can't now."

"It couldn't before," Grace said.

Scott knew from the conviction in her voice, from twenty-five years of marriage, from knowing someone else better than you know yourself, that what she said had to be true.

"Knock, knock." Someone was at the front door.

"Who's there?" Grace asked.

"It's me, Tom," the voice said. "I brought some dessert."

"Tom! You shouldn't have done that." She got up from the floor and stroked her jeans with her hands.

Scott quietly got up and went into the bathroom to wash up.

Grace straightened her hair, hurried to the front door, and opened it wide.

Tom Jackson offered a small package, covered in a checkered cloth.

"Please come in," Grace said.

"It's a blackberry pie," Tom said, handing the gift to Grace. "They grow wild up here."

"Thank you. You shouldn't have."

"Well, I can't take all the credit. I pay the Samford kids. They live in the house at the bottom of the valley. I pay them five dollars a bucket to pick. Then, I just mix them together into a recipe Jenny, my wife, created and pour them in a pie shell."

This was the first time Scott had heard him talk about a wife. He was washing his face. However, the more water he splashed on, the thicker the area around his eyes became. He grabbed a hand towel and wiped his face dry.

"I can smell it from in here," Scott said walking out of the bathroom. "Delicious."

Grace said, "Let's don't wait. Let's have some now." She hustled the pie into the kitchen where she placed it on the table. Scott and Tom walked in behind her and watched as she pulled a knife and some forks from the drawer and sliced the pie into pieces.

"Oh, none for me," Tom said.

"Too late," Grace said, plopping the third slice onto a plate. "Come. Share some with us."

The three gathered around the table.

"Oh, my," Grace said after savoring a bite of the warm pie. "That is wonderful."

183

Scott echoed her sentiment.

"It's a good recipe," Tom said humbly.

They ate in silence, savoring each delectable morsel.

"Your wife must be a wonderful cook," Grace said.

"She was the best," Tom said, pausing between bites.

"What happened?"

"An accident. Three years ago. She was driving home from the store during a heavy snowfall and the truck slipped off the side into a ravine. It took several hours for the authorities to find her. By the time they did, she was comatose. She never came out of it. She died alone," he said. He stopped eating and stared at the kitchen table. "You know, this used to be our table. I moved it up here when I bought this place. I don't need such a large one anymore."

"You're welcome to come up and share this table with us anytime," Grace said reaching over and patting his aged hand.

"Especially if you bring dessert like this," Scott said, trying to add a little levity.

"Thank you," Tom said. "Thank you," he said again and Scott felt he was talking about more than the dessert.

***

The next day, they finished painting the two rooms they were charged with in lieu of rent. Scott took the larger brushes, cans, rollers, and pans to the faucet on the side of the house and washed them clean while Grace touched up one or two spots he had missed. When she finished, she handed him her brush and he washed it as he had done the rest. Then he gathered all of the painting supplies and lugged them down the wooden steps to the driveway and eventually to Tom's house.

Mounting the stairs carefully he tried not to drop any of the clean brushes, cans, or pans. He started to tap on the door to let Tom know he was there when he looked up through the screen and saw the old man sitting by himself in the late afternoon darkness, his head in his hands. Scott backed away from the door carefully.

A large, imposing shadow filled the screen door. "All finished, Scott?" Tom asked.

Scott returned up the porch and handed the painting supplies to him. "Don't know how good it looks, but here's your stuff." Tom's eyes were streaked with red. Their hands brushed softly as Tom accepted the cans and pans and wished Scott a good afternoon.

Scott was disturbed by the sight he had witnessed of Tom just a few moments earlier. He walked over to the edge of the driveway which led out over a huge abyss stretching hundreds of feet down the mountain. Leaning against a hickory tree, absorbing the shade the few leaves left provided, he thought about Tom and what might be on his mind. He wondered what might haunt ministers and who they talk to when they're alone. He had Grace, but Tom didn't seem to have anyone.

Watching the cloud shadows dance over the

valley far away, he let his mind wander. It appeared that the valley was gently changing before his eyes. The land would appear to rise and fall and change shape as the shadows shifted. It seemed alive. A soft breeze passed through his hair, calming him and stirring him at the same time. Somewhere, far down below, music was playing. Its rhythm blended with the cloud shadows in a graceful dance.

A steady beeping sound interrupted the music. Gradually, the music faded and the beeping increased. Muffled voices echoed overhead. Someone nearby, very near, was talking to him. Scott blinked once and he was in a bright, sterile hospital hallway. A doctor, dressed in white coat and striped tie was talking softly outside a patient's room. The name, "Greenwald" was embroidered on his coat. "We've done all we can, Tom. I'm afraid she was too far gone by the time we got to her. Her heart is strong, but there is no brain activity. I'm terribly sorry."

Scott watched, amazed that he could see this vision without medicinal enhancements.

He slowly walked into the room where an older lady lay attached to machines around her. He took Jenny's hand to try to coax life back into her.
"Jenny, I am so sorry I wasn't there. I know it must have been frightening, terribly frightening to be alone. I would do anything to have been with you. Anything."

As he watched, Scott saw the vision change.

The warm, sterile hospital room gave way to a cold, muddy wilderness, surrounded by debris and dirt and grime. The old truck had embedded its bumper deep into the side of the ravine. Jenny sat in the driver's seat. A glance to the mirror revealed a severely bloodied forehead. The window beside her had broken, and cold wind chilled the inside of the car. She tried in vain to push the driver's door open, but she didn't seem to have the strength. She breathed with difficulty. Slowly, her eyes closed and opened again. She looked resolved.

"Hello?" he heard a voice shouting nearby. *"Are you all right?"*

With difficulty, Jenny turned her head and looked toward the sound. There was a person, a man, stumbling down the ravine. He reached the side of the truck, but she could not recognize his face. His clothes indicated he was little more than a homeless vagrant; someone who happened to be on the road when the truck went down.

"I'll go get help," he said.

"No," she answered. "Stay."

He slipped his dirt-smudged arm through the broken window and took her hand. "I'm here, ma'am. But I ain't no doctor. I don't know if I can help you."

"Stay," Jenny said again.

She continued to stare at the homeless man holding her hand. Gradually, the vision faded. The sounds slipped away and she was gone.

***

187

The experience shook Scott like a slap to the face. He backed away from the tree, stumbled over roots and rocks. Gradually, his vision and sense of presence came back. He turned and moved clumsily toward the cabin. Grasping the wooden handrail, he pulled himself upward, mounting each step one at a time. In a daze, he reached the deck and walked around the side, around the back to where Grace was reading a paperback novel.

"Honey?" she said after he staggered onto the back porch. "Are you all right?"

"I honestly don't know," Scott said. He grabbed both arms of the rocking chair and eased his body down into it. A light breeze floated up from the valley and cooled his damp neck.

Grace set her book down and leaned forward. "What happened?"

Scott told her about approaching Tom's home and seeing the figure through the screen door. He also told her about the vision of Tom and Jenny and how the homeless vagrant seemed to comfort her in her final moments. They wondered how the vision could have taken place without medication and assumed Scott had developed the skill after practicing it over and over.

Grace asked, "Should we see someone—get some tests?"

His life was a highway littered with doctors and shrinks whose expertise was never enough. His time with Blackwell was helpful, but Blackwell allowed his darker self to drag Scott into a dangerous world he never wanted to enter again. "Who would we see? We're treading on new territory, here. No one knows how to test for this."

"But what if the medicine caused some sort of serious, permanent damage?"

"Tell you what…if I start dancing naked in the streets, we'll go see a shrink."

"I'd kinda like to see that," Grace said. But the look on her face showed more concern.

***

Late in the day, Scott was sitting in his now favorite rocking chair looking out over his favorite mountain view when Tom Jackson walked around the corner on the cabin's wrap-around deck.

"Busy?" he asked.

"No," Scott answered, then said, "I don't know how you ever pull yourself away from this view. It's stunning."

"That it is," Tom said. "It's almost hypnotic and it never grows old."

"Grace and I certainly do appreciate the chance to use your cabin, Tom."

"It's my pleasure. I'm glad you're enjoying yourselves." He looked about the porch, as if to size up the situation. "Say, I was wondering if I might impose on you for just a little while."

"Sure. What's up?"

"I'm heading into town to get some supplies and stuff and wondered if you'd like to come along."

"Sure."

Scott told Grace he'd be back soon and climbed into Tom's truck. Bouncing down the gravel road, they headed into Waynesville. They passed one sharp turn that skirted a large pine tree on the outside shoulder and a steep drop-off on the inside. Tom seemed to take that particular turn extra slowly. Only after they had passed, did Scott remember that as the place Jenny slipped off the snow-covered road.

Tom's first stop was to get lumber at the building supply and then to head to the grocery store for most of his other things. Scott carried a couple of sacks of groceries and other items for Tom. On their way out, they met a tall barrel-chested man coming in. Scott recognized him instantly from his vision. "Hello, Tom," he said extending his hand warmly. "How are you doing these days?"

"Fine," Tom said while shaking his hand. He turned to introduce Scott.

"Dr. Greenwald," Scott blurted, shaking the doctor's hand. "Nice to meet you."

Tom stopped in his tracks and stared.

As they made their way to the truck, Tom was more quiet than usual. Halfway home, he pulled off the road and asked, "Do you know Dr. Greenwald?"

Scott wasn't sure how to respond. It was a bit like admitting you've been peeping into someone's window at night. On the other hand, it was a legitimate question. He took a deep breath. "Tom, I don't know how you're going to take this, but sometimes I can 'read' other people. I see stories that happened in their lives. Earlier today, I saw an event from yours."

Tom looked puzzled, his forehead wrinkled with valleys.

"I wasn't being nosey. I wasn't searching for something. After I gave you the paint supplies, I was admiring the view from the driveway when it came to me."

"And what did you see?"

"I saw you in the hospital when Dr. Greenwald told you your wife, Jenny, was in a coma."

"How did you know it was Jenny?"

"I heard you say it in the vision."

"Oh my Lord," Tom said, turning away to stare out the windshield.

"You sat on her bed and held her hand and told her you were sorry you weren't with her when she was in the wreck."

Tom's eyes spread wide. He opened his mouth to speak but nothing came out.

"But there's more, Tom," Scott continued. "This has never happened to me before, but right after I saw your vision, I saw another. It was Jenny's. She'd slipped off the road just up ahead, at that tight 'S' curve. It was snowing. Hard."

"That is not possible," Tom muttered, almost a whisper.

"I saw her as she passed," Scott said, feeling compelled to describe it. "Someone, he looked like a drifter or a homeless guy, came down the ravine to try to help her. He stayed with her, holding her hand, until she was gone."

Tom turned and looked into Scott's eyes. "So she wasn't alone?"

Scott shook his head. "She wasn't."

Tears began to spill from Tom's eyes and dampen his wrinkled cheeks. He stayed still for a long time, squeezing the steering wheel gently. "Thank you," he said and quietly put the truck into gear and slowly made his way up the mountain. When they reached the top, he turned to Scott and said, "Let's leave the lumber in the car. I want to be alone for a while." He didn't wait for Scott to get out of the truck, but gathered the grocery sacks and climbed the steps to his house. Transferring all of the bags to one hand, he unlocked and opened his door. He didn't say goodnight.

***

Early the next morning Scott and Grace woke to a gentle knocking on the door of their cabin. Scott scrambled out of bed, pulled on some sweats and rushed to the front door.

"I apologize for waking you," Tom said from the other side of the screen. "I was making some French toast and thought you and Grace might like to join me."

Scott rubbed the sleep from his eyes, blinked a couple of times, and said, "Sure. Give us fifteen minutes and we'll be right over."

He went back to the bedroom and shook Grace awake. They pulled on casual clothes and scrambled down the steps to Tom's house.

Smells of frying bacon and cinnamon French toast lured them up the front steps.

"Come in," Tom called from inside.

The living room was cluttered with cute collectables here and there, mementos from past adventures. A carved wooden bowl containing potpourri took up much of the coffee table. Pillows adorned with knitted designs dotted a long, green sofa. Shelves contained knick-knacks picked up at garage sales and flea markets through the years. A large painting of Tom and Jenny hung from one wall. In one corner, a small TV sat almost hidden from view on an old rolling cart.

"Come on back to the kitchen," Tom yelled.

As they made their way to the back side of the house, the bacon and cinnamon smells became mixed with those of coffee, fried eggs and something almost imperceptible, a hint of vanilla.

"I decided to go hog wild," Tom said. "I haven't made breakfast for anyone in so long, I guess I thought I'd make up for lost time."

They all sat around an old table, filled almost to overflowing with virtually every type of southern breakfast food. The table looked out a side window upon various animal feeders. A bird feeder catered to various species of birds and beyond that, a bird bath offered water. A salt lick was in a clearing a little further out and corn cobs suspended from tree limbs on string tempted squirrels to come by for a bite to eat.

"What a spread," Scott said. "I'm not sure where to begin. You know you're gonna put Waffle House out of business, don't you?"

"Help yourselves to whatever you like," Tom said, waving his hand over the table. He sliced a sliver of butter from the dish and lathered a biscuit. Another chunk and made a pool of butter in the middle of his grits.

Grace accepted a slice of French toast and some

scrambled eggs with a cup of coffee. Scott loaded his plate with some of everything.

Tom ravaged his breakfast like a man rescued from a desert island. "I've gotta tell you," he began. "After talking with you yesterday Scott, I have felt so good, so relieved, so…" he seemed to search for a word, stabbing the air with his fork. "Can you imagine a minister who can't find the right word to say? So redeemed."

"I'm glad to hear that," Scott offered.

"Did he tell you about his visions?" he asked Grace.

She nodded. "Yes, they are a big part of our conversation these days."

"It was incredible. He saw a part of my life, three years ago and recited it back to me as if it had just happened and he had been right there." Then to Scott, "Have you always had them?"

Scott began to relate his recent journey, how he used to have hallucinations, but Dr. Blackwell had helped him control them. He spoke of the tests and trials and then how the ability took them into darkness through cheating and blackmail. He also talked about how he couldn't stop the deaths of Dr. Blackwell or his friends, Jeff, Amy, or Chris.

And then he stopped talking.

They all sipped coffee in silence. Scott breathed in deeply, overwhelmed with thoughts of how his life had changed over the last few months. He felt as if he was in a confessional booth.

"Son," Tom said. "You have a gift, a valuable present from God to truly help others."

And he was feeling stronger. The cool mountain

air, the inspirational scenery, and the deep reflection were working to heal him. "Sometimes it seems like a curse," Scott said.

"The really good ones often do," Tom added.

Eventually, the trio left Tom's kitchen for the porch where they chatted through the morning, sharing story after story, while looking out over the spectacular view of the Great Smokey Mountains. The more Scott talked, the more he felt that his ability just might be a blessing after all.

But he wasn't sure.

CHAPTER FIFTEEN

"Are you up for another errand?" Tom asked Scott the next afternoon.

"What do you have in mind?"

"Just a trip into town," he said, eyes gleaming as if electrically charged.

Scott knew from his evasiveness that he had something up his sleeve, but Tom had let them stay in his cabin and Scott and Grace weren't doing much more than sitting in rocking chairs on the porch. Besides, he did enjoy these jaunts with the wild preacher man. "Sure, but do you think the grocery store can handle us two days in a row?"

"Oh, we aren't going there," Tom said.

They boarded the truck and headed back down the mountain. It seemed that Tom took the curve where Jennie had slid off the mountain just a little faster than the day before. Perhaps he was a little more comfortable than he had been previously.

They drove past Waynesville and on into Maggie Valley where they stopped at St. Joseph's hospital, a utilitarian, two story building surrounded by blacktop parking lots and small, trim trees and bushes.

Tom turned to Scott and said, "From time to time, I drop in here for a visit. Join me." More of a command than an invitation.

They walked through sliding glass doors and Tom checked in at the front desk. The volunteers instantly recognized him as he did them. "I see you're back from your trip to Florida, Carolyn. How are the grandchildren? Betty, have you lost weight? You look great." Somehow, the towering preacher made even the simplest inquiries seem sincere. He took time to introduce Scott to each person, as if introducing his best friend. The two men continued their journey into the small hospital, visiting patients and medical staff and taking time to listen to each one.

In one warmly decorated room, walls adorned with countless coloring pictures of children playing, they met Katie. She lay in bed watching TV, her bald head resting against a large Sponge Bob Square Pants pillow. She was tiny and the cancer had taken so much from her frail body that she looked half her age.

When Tom walked in the door, Scott saw a minute sparkle in her eyes. Her lips curled into a half smile.

"Hello, sweetheart," Tom bellowed in his most enthusiastic voice. "How is my favorite little lady?"

Katie didn't say anything but allowed him to reach down into the bed and scoop her into his arms so he could give her a massive hug. She hugged him back as strongly as her thin arms could and laid her head against his broad shoulder.

A nurse rushed in behind Scott. "Now take it easy, Rev. Jackson. You're gonna break something if you ain't careful."

But Tom hugged her like she was his own. "I've got someone I want you to meet," he said and Katie turned her gaze to Scott.

"This is my friend, Mr. Scott," Tom said in southern colloquial lingo.

Katie slowly climbed down off Tom's arms and onto the antiseptically clean tile floor. She stood tentatively beside the bed and looked at the corner of the room, as if not sure what to do or say.

"Hi, Katie," Scott offered. He crouched down on his haunches so he was close to her height, but she didn't look at him. "It's so nice to meet you. How old are you?"

Katie did not respond.

Her hesitation was as obvious as her naked head so he, too, wrapped a long arm around her waist.

"Mr. Scott, have you ever seen a more beautiful little girl?"

"No, I can't say that I ever have," Scott said. Still she kept her gaze on the corner of the room. She looked so frail, Scott feared she might break if he stared at her too much, so he turned his attention elsewhere.

"Hey, that's Donald Duck," he said, looking at the television screen.

Katie slowly turned her head to the TV.

"I used to watch Donald Duck when I was your age," Scott said. "He was one of my favorites." Then, in an effort to make her smile, he added,

"You are forty-two, aren't you?"

Katie shook her head but still remained silent.

"We'd better let you get some rest," Tom said and lifted her back into bed. "Are you still my girlfriend?" he asked and she half-smiled again. Tom stroked her cheek with a thick hand.

When they stepped back into the hallway, the nurse followed them out the door. "She loves to have you come visit," she told Tom. "And I know bringing a friend was a real treat for her today," she said to Scott.

"How's she doing?" Tom asked.

The nurse shook her head. "Her doctors have tried everything," she said. "Yesterday they told her mama she wasn't going to live much longer and her mama told Katie. She hasn't spoken since." Her voice quivered as she studied the tile floor.

The news, in all its naked cruelty shook Scott as if it had been conveyed directly to him.

The two men continued their Florence Nightingale duties, visiting an old man who kept asking Tom for a cigarette, an obese woman who nearly flowed off the sides of the bed, and a ten year old boy who had broken both legs when he fell out of a tree house. They all knew Tom.

Back in the truck, Tom turned to Scott. "I'm not sure how, but I believe your presence might be a blessing to some of those people in the hospital. That's why I asked you here."

"Tom," Scott said. "I don't know how to help those people."

"Son, I've been in the ministry for fifty years and most of the time I don't know how to help the people I serve. But I try anyway and yet somehow, someone walks away a better person. You'll figure it out," Tom sighed and started the engine.

Scott rode in silence all the way back to the cabin.

***

"All right," Scott said. "I'll give it a shot."

Tom had been telling Grace all about their hospital visit. He mentioned the boy with two broken legs and the obese lady and several other patients by name. He seemed to be taking a long time to get around to Katie, and Scott sensed that was his way of persuading him to offer to do a reading. "I know where you're going, Tom," Scott said eventually. "If I don't do something, you'll probably still be here talking to us when the sun comes up."

Tom blushed, his agenda exposed. "I believe you can somehow help those people."

Scott turned and stepped out to the back porch. Rocking in one of the chairs, he began to relax. Through the screen door, he heard Grace offer Tom a glass of iced tea. In a few moments they quietly walked out onto the porch to watch Scott.

"You don't have to tip-toe," Scott said. "I know you're here."

With that, Scott began to describe each vision. He talked about significant events from staff members and patients. He told them one patient had once played minor league baseball and another had fought in Vietnam and that a kid who fell out of the treehouse and broke both legs would have a few more accidents later in his life.

Then he said, "Oh, this is what I think you're looking for."

Grace and Tom moved closer as if concerned they might miss something.

"I'm pretty sure I've found Katie's stories," Scott said. He was staring out over the valley, trance-like. "Now this is interesting. Katie has several episodes or memories, like many other people. However, most of hers, in fact, all but one, seem to be faded. It's like they have started to disappear, like Blackwell's did, but more slowly."

"Oh, my," Scott heard Grace say.

"Here's one. It shows a lady, could be Katie as an adult, holding an infant. It looks like a newborn baby. I'll try another one." He sighed deeply. "Oh, here's an interesting view. Apparently Katie has an interest in music. She's in an orchestra, playing, uh, violin, or viola. Dang, it sounds pretty good."

"Well, her daddy used to play a fiddle with a bluegrass band over in Cullowhee," Tom whispered to Grace.

"Let me take a look at the one that seems most intact," Scott said. "I'm assuming this means the event has already happened. The others may be in danger of never occurring."

Tom leaned back against the rail and Grace sat in a vacant rocking chair.

"I hear hospital noises," Scott said. "You know, loudspeaker voices, beeping sounds, echoes. Okay, the vision is opening up. Katie's in bed and talking with someone. The TV is on in the background. Oh, she's talking with you, Tom. It's your ugly mug. She's giggling. She seems so incredibly happy. I can't tell what you've said to her, but something makes her laugh."

Scott turned his head to face Tom. Great tears rolled down the man's weathered cheeks. All at once, he sniffed deeply. "My Lord. I never…"

"You did, Tom," Scott said.

"You got me crying like a bride at a wedding," Tom said. He went back into the bathroom. In a moment, they heard a loud honk as he blew his nose.

Scott slid back into his meditative position and breathed in deeply, again. In a moment, he seemed to find something else. "Here's something. Katie seems to be with an older man. It's Dr. Greenwald. They're in a clinic of some type. Hmm. I'll look for some indication…oh, a logo says, 'Charles Wesley Cancer Center of Oregon.' There's a thin man, looks like he's from India. He's greeting Dr. Greenwald and Katie. He's wearing a name tag; Dr. Kapur. Greenwald looks very pleased and Katie is hugging Dr. Kapur."

Tom had returned from the bathroom and now stood in the doorway.

"Now, Katie's back in Waynesville. It looks like she's getting off a school bus and her mother is running to greet her. She has something in her hand—a paper, no, a letter. Her mother is saying the cancer is in total remission and Dr. Kapur's treatments seem to have worked. Mom's crying. Katie's crying. Good God, even the bus driver is crying."

Scott came out of the vision. "Does that mean Dr. Kapur has a cure?"

Tom said, "Sounds 'bout like it. I need to find out more about this guy."

"That means there's hope for Katie," Scott echoed.

"That means there's hope for us all," Grace said.

***

Tom was off on a mission, trying to find information about Dr. Kapur, the Charles Wesley Cancer Center of Oregon and attempting to connect that doctor and facility with Dr. Greenwald at St. Joseph's Hospital in Maggie Valley.

Grace and Scott were alone for the evening. They fixed a simple spaghetti dinner with a salad and then pulled the kitchen table to the porch so they could watch the sun set fire to the mountains while they ate. Crickets had come out to sing together across the valley. Scott poured a red wine and they toasted the valley, their marriage, and his gift. In the relative silence of the evening, three young deer waltzed through the back yard to feed on corn Tom had laid out hours earlier.

It was the perfect time.

Grace stood up, kissed him warmly on the lips, gathered the dishes, and took them inside. He could hear her washing them in the sink.

He leaned back in the rocking chair and thought about the woman who had stayed by his side through thick and thin for so many years. The chirping crickets raised their rhythmic song and sounded almost metallic. Then, the chatter moved to somewhere over his head and behind him.

The vision cleared and he recognized the gangway of an aerial tramway heading up a tree-lined ravine in Wyoming.

He remembered the event as if it were yesterday, but in fact it was one of their first vacations three years after their wedding. Grace had clung to him all the way up the mountain, which seemed odd to Scott since both were at the mercy of the tram and gravity. Had there been any danger, he wouldn't have been any safer than she.

In an instant the creaky sound of the tram faded and he felt his body moving back and forth to big band music. A mirror ball rotated overhead. Formal-clad employees from the hospital where she worked danced the swing. Grace held his hand tightly with one hand and his side with the other. They jitter-bugged through the night, although neither was an accomplished dancer. The others in the massive ballroom, celebrating some all-employee nonsense or another, were all face-less and long forgotten. To Grace, the only person on the floor was Scott.

The music changed again to soft and inaccurate guitar picking. Scott must have been under twenty, sitting on the grass at the university, playing soft-rock songs on a badly-tuned guitar. Students walked by on the sultry spring evening oblivious to his music and even more oblivious to his off-key notes.

But Grace listened intently, soaking in the song as if it were pitch-perfect and inspirational.

That was the first night they kissed and he played for her every night for a month afterwards.

The sound of his out-of-tune guitar faded away, and soft elevator music came down from above. When his vision cleared, Scott was surprised to see they were actually riding in an elevator, going down to the parking garage five or six flights below in the medical complex. The walls of the elevator contained large mirrors and he saw that his own eyes were red and bloodshot. Again, Grace had a short arm around his waist to support him in a tough time.

"It's all right," she said.

"No, you've always wanted children and I'll never be able to give them to you," he choked.

"I will always love you," she whispered.

Her whispers faded back to the sound of mountain crickets. The sun had not fully set and would be up for just a few more seconds. Grace place an aged hand on his, holding it as warmly and tenderly as ever. But her hand was wrinkled and spotted, just like his own skin. He realized they were back in the mountains, only years into the future and were sharing another mountain sunset from their back porch.

The scene slowly changed, but Scott couldn't tell if he was still in the vision or not. The mountains lay out before him. The sun was almost gone. The cool breeze kissed his face. Grace walked out the back door and proclaimed, "I do love this view."

Scott stood up, turned around, and pulled his wife to him. He kissed her deeply.

"Okay, Scotty," she said. "I'll do the dishes every night if I get this kind of a response from you."

"I love you," he said, as he realized all her fully-lived moments were with him. Through the years she supported him, loved him, and helped him without so much as a request that he return the favor. He had, however, but her selfless love never insisted nor demanded that he do so. It was just a natural response.

They kissed again and he signaled his passion by slipping his tongue between her moist lips.

"Mmm," she said, urging him on.

"I so love you," he said after they broke apart.

"I love you," she said.

When his hands slid down her side to her waist and then further to her buttocks, she pressed herself to him. And when his knee slid in between hers, she accommodated him by spreading her legs a little wider apart. In moments, they were dancing, probably to the rhythm of the crickets, but definitely to their own rising passion. He felt his leg brush her sensitive area over and over and realized with pleasure she wanted him, needed him there.

Their passion rose and he carried her back to the bedroom and laid her down on the soft bed flanked by naked logs on all corners. She gasped at each button as he unbuttoned her blouse. She arched her back and allowed him to slide her panties down.

She sought his jeans and reached inside to massage and stroke and prepare him for her. Through it all, her lips never left his, not even when she panted hard and gasped for air.

Then, their sweaty bodies parted in exhaustion and they lay on a bed blessed with moonlight through a large window that looked out to the view they had watched earlier that evening.

Scott reminded himself of one of the only nice things about his being sterile. When they made love, neither worried about contraception, but both loved without bounds.

"You know," he said after his breath came back to him. "We're going to retire up here one day."

"I know," she answered. "You just realized that?"

"I saw it," he said.

"I knew it the first day we arrived," she responded.

***

"Scott! Grace!" Pounding on the cabin door heightened the urgency of the call.

Scott leapt from the bed, dragged on a shirt and sweat pants and ran to the living room. Tom Jackson stood outside the front door.

"What's happening?" Scott asked after yanking open the door.

"We need your help," Tom answered. "Old Ray Sawyer is missing. We're forming a search party."

"Let me get Grace," Scott said, welcoming Tom into the living room.

The trio dashed down to Tom's truck and sped into town. A light mist floated over parts of the mountain road, causing Tom to slow the truck, and draping the mission in mysterious danger.

On the drive in, Tom explained the situation. "Ray's almost as old as these mountains. Lived at one of the old houses constructed in the sixties just off Main Street. A couple a years ago he was diagnosed with Alzheimer 's disease, and he's gone down quickly ever since."

Tom slowed to maneuver a turn and then added, "Ray's a good ole' boy. He just gets real confused these days. His son, Jerry, along with Patti, Jerry's wife, moved in with him when he was diagnosed, to look after him. But, somehow Ray slipped out the back door a couple of nights ago when Jerry and Patti were in bed, and nobody's seen him since."

Grace asked, "Was the house locked up securely?"

"Jerry said the back door was unlocked. He must have accidentally left it that way before he went to bed."

A small crowd was gathering at the courthouse when Grace, Scott, and Tom rounded the corner. Before they exited the truck, Scott requested they keep his abilities a secret. "Let's not say anything about seeing the future or reading people's minds, or anything like that, okay?"

Tom instantly said, "Of course. I'll do my best." He parked in a small parking lot across the street from the courthouse. As they climbed down from Tom's truck, Scott noticed a couple arguing in the courthouse parking lot. "Who's that?" he asked

Tom.

"Oh, that's Jerry and Patti."

The trio paused briefly to watch the confrontation from afar.

"I wanna help with the search," Patti said.

"Git on back to the house. He may come wandering back home," Jerry retorted.

"He ain't coming home and you know it," Patti said.

"That ain't true woman," Jerry insisted. "You'll see. We'll find him. If it ain't today, might be tomorrow. But daddy's gonna come home."

"Wake up and smell the coffee. He ain't—"

"Stop that kinda talk right now and git on home," Jerry interrupted. "I'll catch a ride with Donnie after the search is over."

Patti stared at him a moment before complying and driving away in a run-down Chevy.

Scott, Grace, and Tom joined the small crowd at the steps of the courthouse where the local sheriff was addressing the crowd. "Ray's been out for 'bout three days, now," he said. "Unless he hitched a ride, which is a tad doubtful, he can't be too far away. He may be sleeping in some culvert or walking around in someone's back yard. We've just got to spread out and see if we can find out where he is." He handed out photographs of Ray. "If you'll turn these over, you'll see a full description of the individual. He's six feet, one inch tall. He is balding with gray hair around the side and back of his head and he has brown eyes. He is confused easily, but may answer to the name, 'Ray.' If you find him, just stay with him and call me. We'll come to you and pick him up. Are there any questions?"

"Is he dangerous?" a man near the front of the crowd asked.

"No," the sheriff said. "He's probably pretty tame, however, like most people, if he is confused or startled, he might react."

"Is there a reward?" another asked.

"The county is offering a five-hundred-dollar reward to the first person who finds Ray."

A few people in the crowd grumbled. "Is that all?" One short, skinny guy who looked like he desperately needed a makeover, asked.

"I heard he got sixty grand from the insurance company after his wife died. All you can muster up is five hundred dollars?" Another guy asked.

"Now you know, Bobby, that money is all tied up in the will," the Sheriff said. As if on cue, he turned to Jerry who had just walked up. "Do you want to add anything?"

Jerry seemed a bit sedated. "Ah, you probably covered it all."

"Okay," the sheriff said. "Bob, why don't you take a handful of folks and spread out north on Highway twenty-three. Bill, you go in the opposite direction. Sarah-Jane, you and a couple of people go west on Little Mountain Road, and Jerry and I will go east on Hazelwood. If you see or hear anything, call me on my cell. The number's on the back of your photographs."

Scott stood at the back of the crowd and watched the volunteers. No one acted suspicious. No one acted strange.

Grace asked, "Well, should we join one of the search teams to get a better look?"

Tom seemed to consider hailing one of the group leaders, but then turned back to Scott and Grace. "You know, Jerry's wife went back to the house. Maybe we should check on her, first."

"That might seem kinda suspicious," Scott said.

"Don't you do pastoral visits?" Grace asked.

"She's a Baptist," Tom muttered. "I'm Methodist."

"Well, we'll just have to go as concerned neighbors," Grace offered.

They loaded back into the truck, drove out of the parking lot, and headed toward Ray's house. On the way they stopped at the local Piggly-Wiggly and bought a casserole to bring with them.

Patti's Chevy was parked under an oak tree at the edge of the driveway. Ray's house was a small, nondescript, clapboard structure, similar to many constructed around the mid '60s. The front porch overlooked a yard, apparently once adorned with ornamental flowers and bushes, but now overgrown with weeds. Tom led Grace up the three short steps onto the porch and rapped on the screen door. Scott hesitated, waiting by the truck.

Grace turned and waved him forward.

Feeling like they were imposing on someone who obviously had a lot to do at the moment, Scott wanted to call the whole thing off and go back to the cabin. But then, he got a closer look at Patti.

***

She looked whipped. She stared through the screen door, eyes buried deep in their sockets, shoulders slumped, and hands twisting a worn-out dishtowel. Even through the rusty screen door, Scott could see a red welt on her arm. "Yes?"

"Good morning, Mrs. Sawyer. I'm Rev. Tom Jackson. I'm a retired minister. My friends, Scott and Grace and I just wanted to drop by and share our thoughts and prayers with you."

Grace stepped forward and extended the casserole like a prized gift. "Oh," Tom added. "We brought a little something to help you through this tough time."

Patti opened the door a crack and gratefully accepted the casserole dish.

"Would you like to join us on the porch?" Tom asked, sweeping a hand toward the rocking chairs.

"I guess," Patti said. She quickly added, "But I do…" and turned to look inside as if to retract her acceptance.

Tom interceded, "We'll only stay a minute." Scott held the screen door open for her and patted her lightly on the shoulder as she walked to the porch. Patti took the chair closest to the door and Grace and Tom carefully descended into the other two, somewhat rickety chairs. Scott moved to the end of the porch and sat down on the floor, leaning against one of the posts.

"How are you holding up?" Tom began.

"Well," she answered. "You know…it's hard, especially since you don't know if he'll ever come back…or when."

"I understand," Tom reassured.

Scott stared down at the dirt at the base of the porch and let Tom's voice slip away as he focused on Patti. Tracing patterns in the dirt with his shoe, he slipped into a vision-state, cautious of what he might find there.

"I don't care for all the attention," Patti continued. "The search parties and the phone calls in the middle of the night."

Scott saw several of Patti's vision-windows. He slipped in and out of them, one at a time.

She was playing with a little girl on a playground on a bright, sunny day. She stood before the altar with Jerry on their wedding day. Then he found more than what he was searching for.

An older man, strongly resembling the picture of Ray Sawyer the Sheriff passed out earlier, was standing in the doorway of the house they were now visiting. "Where is it," he shouted. His left hand gripped the doorframe. "Woman, I ain't gonna ask you again. Where is my wife's picture?"

"I ain't seen it, Ray. Did you look in your bedroom?" He heard her say in a trembling voice.

"It ain't there, 'cause you took it. You took it...like you took my home and like you're gonna take my life insurance money," Ray shouted.

"I wouldn't do that," Patti plead.

"You and that no-good son of mine are stealing it all." He came toward her with glaring eyes.

Patti held her arms before her like a boxer guarding his head from coming punches.

Ray swung his right hand, finding cheek beyond her protective arms and she slipped, falling hard to the wood floor.

"You're gonna learn a lesson, bitch!" He kicked at her, but she scrambled away.

"No! Don't!" she cried and rolled over. On hands and knees she tried to crawl away.

Ray reached down to his waist and unbuckled his belt. "You can't get away from me."

The first lash slashed her slender back, sending bolts of pain through her skin. Scott winced in pain. *A scream ruptured from deep in her belly in response. She gasped to suck in air when the second belt lash, this one harder than the first, sliced across her skin. She desperately tried to crawl faster, but Ray stayed atop her. Timing her getaway as well as she could, Patti jerked to the right when she thought Ray would strike again. Her instincts were close and his belt glanced off her left side, ripping down her hips and buttocks.*

"God damn it!" he shouted.

Patti scrambled faster, trying to reach the screen door to the back porch and safety.

She heard the swish of the belt as Ray swung again and jerked to her left, hoping to dodge the deadly leather. But her movement wasn't fast enough and the strap found its mark, sending stabbing pain through her arm. This time a guttural wail passed her lips and she body-rolled toward the door. When her back hit the floor, striking pain from the floggings shot through her, reigniting the numbing torture.

"You never learn, do you?" Ray shouted.

"No!" she managed to shout, backing away on all fours crab-walk style.

Just then lights panned the dining room wall behind them and the creak of Jerry's rickety Chevy over the loose gravel in the driveway interrupted the assault. Ray hastily dropped his belt and turned toward the living room to meet his son. He turned back to Patti and cautioned, "One word of this and I'll beat the hell out of you." He closed the door securely behind him.

Patti could hear the two men talking casually in the next room. She pulled herself up to a sitting position and leaned against the kitchen wall. She gasped for fresh air and hugged her knees to her body. Vengeance replaced the fear in her soul. It was over. The terrible ordeal was over. But things were about to get worse.

***

"Excuse me, sir," Patti said, her face just a few inches from Scott's. She was leaning over to get his attention, offering a cup of lemonade. "Would you like something to drink?"

Scott looked up to see Grace and Tom sipping on their own cups of the tart brew. "It's quite good," Tom said.

Scott looked to Grace who could not be seen by Patti. She wrinkled her face sending a non-verbal message of disdain.

"Oh, uh, sure," Scott said, reaching up and accepting the cup. Apparently, Patti had brought out a pitcher of the refreshing drink while Scott was watching her visions.

She smiled pleasantly and then returned to the

chair she had occupied earlier. "Where were we?"

"Uh," Tom muttered. "You were telling us how you and Jerry met."

Hidden from Patti's view behind the porch pole, Scott poured most of the lemonade onto the ground at his feet. He set the cup down and quietly slipped back into his trance. In his earlier vision he had seen something that scared him—made him want to look further. He skimmed past the childhood memories, past the violent encounter with Ray and into a nighttime experience.

Patti slipped out of the bed well after midnight. She quietly dressed in a sweatshirt and jeans and tiptoed down the hall to Ray's room. Leaning over his bed, she shook the old man awake. "Ray. Ray. Wake up."

"Huh? Who is that? Darlene?"

"No, it's Patti. But it's time to go see Darlene," she said.

Ray sat up in bed and Patti helped him dress in slacks, a shirt, and his bedroom slippers.

"Where's Darlene?" he said, a little too loud.

"Shhh, Ray." Patti said. "I'll take you to see her." Patti took Ray's arm and walked him toward the back door. She carefully scaled the steps to the grass below.

Scott noticed Patti seemed completely emotionless, as if she were following a script and not acting on feeling.

The odd pair, he a full foot taller than she and

dressed in pajamas, and she struggling to push him along, stumbled around the outside of the house to Jerry's beat-up Chevy. Patti helped him climb into the passenger side of the car, saying, "We're gonna see Darlene."

"Darlene?"

"Yes," Patti reassured him. "Very soon."

The car fired up and Patti felt a shock of fear that Jerry might wake up at that sound. She backed out of the driveway, lights off.

"Where is she?" Ray said, looking around the car quickly.

"She's waiting for you, Ray. Up ahead."

They drove on for thirty minutes, or so, into the curvy roads of the Great Smokey Mountain National Park. Eventually, Patti pulled off the main highway and onto a small, dirt lane, marked by a lone sign that said, "Park Personnel Only." About two hundred yards in she stopped the car before a metal gate blocking the road. "C'mon, Ray. We're almost there."

Ray opened the door quickly, looking down the dirt lane beyond the gate. "Darlene is there?"

"That's right, Ray," Patti said. "She's just a little way up ahead."

Ray cautiously stepped from the vehicle as if he were stepping from a boat into murky water. He looked back at Patti one more time and then turned and walked up the road and past the closed gate.

Patti put the car in reverse and backed down the road a few feet.

Ray stopped and turned to look after her as the car backed away.

She forced herself to focus on the road behind her and backed further, quickly. At one point, the right side of the car screeched into a hedge of thick bushes, scraping the rear fender. "Shit," she exclaimed. She jammed the car in drive, rumbled forward, and then backed up again, this time steering the trunk of the car to the right to avoid the bushes. She missed them by inches.

Her last vision was of Ray standing alone behind the metal gate, looking after her. He reminded her of the puppies at the Pet Rescue Center in Canton and how they stared after her when she visited. The image of Ray burned into her mind and melted her heart. Tears began to flow. She could barely see the dirt road through the wash of tears. When she reached the turnoff from the highway, she backed the car around so she could enter driving forward. She ratcheted the gear into Park and broke down crying. Over and over she told herself, "This is the best thing. This is the best thing." She tried to look on the bright side—to remind herself that Ray had been abusive and to think about the sixty-thousand-dollar insurance policy. She pounded the steering wheel, wishing for another way out but knowing none existed.

After a devastating twenty minutes of emotional torment, she surfaced exhausted and emotionless. Pulling the gearshift to "D," she eased the car out onto the asphalt road and headed for home.

Scott backed out of the vision and opened his eyes. Patti and Tom were chatting about small things—gossip, mostly, about people in the community. Grace was watching him intently. He returned the look and then slowly nodded.

"Uh, Tom," Grace said. "Don't forget we have to meet your friends for lunch," she said, alerting him that Scott had completed his process.

The trio thanked Patti for her time and politely left.

"What did you see?" Grace insisted as soon as the truck doors had slammed shut. "C'mon. Don't hold out."

Tom, who had cranked the engine, waited patiently to hear Scott's response.

"Guys," Scott began. "We need to go someplace where we can talk. I need to concentrate."

So, they drove on in silence. Grace and Tom seemed impatiently quiet while Scott was deep in thought. He wondered how they were going to handle this.

***

The odd trio walked along the sidewalks of downtown Waynesville, glancing here and there in quaint shops and cafés. The cool mountain air helped clear Scott's head. He used that time to review all that he had just witnessed through Patti's visions.

"We've got a bit of a dilemma," he started.

"Was she involved?" Grace asked.

"Oh, yeah. She did it," Scott said. "She took him up into the Smokies, dropped him off, and drove away."

"Are you sure she didn't go back to get him?"

"I think there'd be a vision for that and I didn't see it," Scott said. "It really broke her up. She took it hard."

"We'd better contact the sheriff," Grace said.

"I'm not so sure," Scott said. "He's been out there for three days. Odds are he fell down a cliff or was attacked by wild animals."

Tom and Grace stared at Scott. "How can you be so insensitive?" Grace insisted.

"Because I saw more," he said. He stopped and turned directly to Grace. "He beat her," he said. "I don't know how often—I only saw one episode. But I saw him take off his belt and attack her mercilessly."

His words caused Grace to pause.

"Are you sure this wasn't one of the visions that doesn't come true?" Tom asked. "I never knew Ray to be violent."

"No, I'm not sure this one really happened. But I did see what I thought looked like a welt on her right arm this morning."

"You know, brain injury people and Alzheimer's victims sometimes act violently. I've seen it at the hospital, especially when they are confused."

"In the vision, he claimed she took a photograph of his wife. I doubt that she ever did, but someone like Ray might react harshly in a situation like that."

"So do we tell the sheriff?" Grace asked.

"That's the dilemma," Scott said. "I am ninety-nine percent sure this event took place and it may have been somewhat justified. But, we can't tell anyone."

"Why not?" Tom asked. "She committed a

serious crime."

"Because no one will believe us," Scott answered. "Do we go to the police and say, 'I had a vision in which Patti drove Ray out to the mountains and left him?' Who would believe us?"

They all let Scott's words settle in like a thick fog on a cool night. "No one would believe us," he added to emphasize the numbing fact. He looked at the little town about him. The quaint shops and cafés of Waynesville had lost their attraction— despair can have that effect.

"Anyone want some coffee?" Tom asked.

"Chocolate ice cream is my usual pick-me-up in times like this," Grace added.

"I'll take beer, even though it's not yet noon," Scott added.

"Wait a minute," Tom said.

"You want a beer?" Scott asked.

"No, something better," Tom said with a gleam in his eye. "We leave a note. We write a message, anonymously, for the sheriff and tell him where Ray was dropped off."

"That might work," Scott said. He looked to Grace for a response.

"Do we mention Patti?"

"I say, 'no'," Tom said. "I don't see any good that will come of it."

"And, she may have been justified in doing it," Scott added.

They bought a cheap notepad at one of the shops and crafted a nondescript, anonymous note to the sheriff, which said:

Ray Sawyer was taken into the Smokey Mountains three nights ago and left near Stevens Creek Rd. If you search that area, you will probably find him.

They drove to the Haywood County Sheriff's office and quietly slipped the note under the windshield of one of the vehicles in the back parking lot.

"And now, we wait," Tom said matter-of-factly as they drove away.

And waiting is always the hardest thing to do.

***

The next morning, Scott checked the news from a local web site. Old Ray Sawyer had been found in a ravine near Stevens Creek Road. An anonymous tip led those in a search party to the body. It looked like Ray had fallen into the ravine and broken his neck a couple of days earlier. Wild animals had recently disturbed the body. A post to the article indicated some people were disappointed that the five hundred dollar reward would not be given to those involved in the search.

Their time in the mountains at an end, Scott and Grace packed the Prius. Gumby took one more long sniff around the woods and bounded over to the car, ready to head home.

Tom closed the front door on his house and approached the Moores. "I'm sure gonna miss you three," he said.

Scott walked around to say goodbye. "We were just coming to see you," he said.

"I wanted you to know the latest about Katie," Tom said. "Dr. Greenwald managed to get some information on The Charles Wesley Cancer Institute. It sounds like Dr. Kapur and his staff are doing some amazing work treating cancer among children. And they invited Katie to come out for a consultation."

Grace said, "That's wonderful news."

"Yes, it is. The only thing is the treatment is expensive."

"Just tell a few of your friends up here and take some donations," Scott said. "Pass the plate. Every preacher I've ever met knows how to do that."

"Some say that's all we know how to do," Tom laughed. After a moment of thought, he added, "I've been thinking about your visions. They seem to be about the really important experiences in peoples' lives. Like the people I've talked with who died and came back—they remember the important ones— those that seem to pass before their eyes." He looked directly at Scott. "That's what you see."

"That sounds deep," Scott said.

"I want you to feel free to come back anytime, ya' hear?"

The three hugged in the driveway. Gumby barked from the back seat.

Grace and Scott climbed in their car and left for home.

CHAPTER SIXTEEN

When they arrived home, Grace dropped Scott, Gumby, and their luggage at the driveway before backing out to pick up a few items at the grocery store. Scott was dragging the bags and the leashed dog through the front door when he was startled by a familiar, haunting voice. "Hello, Scott. Did you have a nice trip?"

Gumby lunged against the leash, barking and growling, causing Scott to drop his luggage.

He turned to look directly into the face of Paul Blackwell who was sitting in the living room on the same sofa where Kathy Becker sat several months earlier. He held a pistol in his lap pointed in Scott's direction. Beneath dark sunglasses Scott could see scars and scabs over the left side of his face. Next to the chair, a cane lay on the floor.

"Hold on tightly to that leash," Dr. Blackwell said. "I wouldn't want your dog to get hurt."

"You're alive?"

"Very much so, thanks to the skill of a couple of EMTs and a defibrillator in the ambulance,"

Blackwell said. Then, with a bit more urgency added, "You'd better put that mutt away or this gun might accidentally discharge."

Scott did as he was told and locked the dog in the kitchen. "Why are you here?" he asked.

"Simple. I wanted to check on my experiment," he said.

"I'm not an experiment," Scott said.

"Oh, I beg to differ."

"I'm tired of your games. I'm ready to move on with my life," Scott said defiantly. "I imagine my brother was, as well."

"Oh, you found out about your twin."

"I found out you killed him," Scott said.

"It was such a shame. He was doing quite well until he tired of the drugs and the exercises."

"You are a despicable, pathetic man. I hope you rot in Hell."

"I believe I have already begun the process," Blackwell said. He slowly removed his sunglasses to reveal an eye-less socket, distorted and hollow and grotesque.

Scott flinched. "What do you want, Blackwell?"

"What I've worked for years to get."

"All right. I'll work with you. Publish your damn papers or write your reports or whatever. You can blackmail whoever you want. Get your goddamn special award for your work in paranormal research. Whatever. Then we go our separate ways."

"At one time that may have sufficed. But, a couple of weeks ago I sustained some deep, painful, and costly injuries. My doctor bills are enormous and will only increase with time, so I require much more to take care of myself." He wiped some drainage beneath the place where his left eye had been.

"I don't think I can help with that."

"Oh, I think you can," Blackwell said.

"And if I refuse?"

"I'll kill you and then come back here and kill your wife and then kill your damn dog…but not in that order."

"And if I help you get the money for your…injuries, you'll leave us alone?"

"Oh, no, Scott," Blackwell said. "As I mentioned, that is not enough."

Blackwell's games infuriated Scott. "What the hell do you want?" he yelled.

"I want your abilities. I want to learn exactly what happened to you and how to replicate that. Then I can enhance others' abilities to obtain any information I want."

"Impossible."

"Oh, I think it's very possible," Blackwell added.

"What are you talking about?" Scott asked. "That could take years."

Blackwell smiled a wounded, crooked smile. "Ah, but you forget, my friend. I have already been working on this process for many years. I'm very close. You hold the key to completing my studies."

"What if you can't do it? What if you fail to create your magic pill."

"I don't fail very often," Blackwell countered.

"You failed with my brother," Scott said.

Blackwell stared him down with his one eye. "Your brother failed me."

"And what if I refuse?" Scott asked.

"Scott, I'm making you an offer you cannot refuse," he said.

"I'm not a guinea pig."

"Yes, you are." His voice rose in intensity. "You are to blame for this," he said, waving his hand across his face. "You owe me, you freak of nature."

Scott felt his shoulders slump. He had no choice.

***

"It is good that your wife didn't come inside with you," Blackwell said as he led Scott to his black BMW, which was parked a block up the street. "She will return only to find you are missing. If you can't help me, you will never be found."

Scott sat in the passenger's seat, a small suitcase containing a change of clothes between his feet. "Where are we going?"

"You know I can't tell you that, Scott. It would be better that you not ask such questions." He was leaning into the car through the open passenger window. Scott could see his ravaged goatee up close and it wasn't pretty.

"Just curious, you know?"

"Curiosity killed the cat and your dog," he said with a touch of venom.

"If I cooperate with you and you create your super drug so you can make super-psychics out of anyone you want, will you leave me alone?"

"Of course, Scott. If others can read people as you do, why would I need you?" His words left a chilling effect. "Besides, I don't like having you

227

around. You talk too much."

Scott was looking out the window to his home, wondering how Grace would take his absence when Blackwell quickly reached in and injected something into his neck with a small hypodermic needle. Everything went black.

CHAPTER SEVENTEEN

Some teenage kids were laughing and teasing. Someone pushed him about. Another boy knocked his glasses off his face and someone else smashed them with the heel of his boot. An older boy started to punch Him. He realized he was aiming for the most vulnerable parts of the body—the eyes and the nose. His shoes slipped on the wet, slimy pavement and he fell to the ground.

He covered his head with his arms and the older boy started kicking him with pointed boots. His ribs hurt like hell. "You're just a pussy," the older boy shouted. One boot landed in a soft spot near his ear, knocking him over on his side. He didn't move. He didn't open his eyes. One by one the other children left. The big boy landed one more boot to his head and then marched away, victorious.

The dream morphed into another.

His head whipped forward as a thick hand slapped it hard. The slap was familiar. After all, it happened every time he did something stupid.

"Are you playing with girls again," his father teased. "Are you growing up to be a little girly boy? Can't you play with boys your age? Talk to me, girly boy!"

But he couldn't. When his father got this way, he couldn't say a thing. His throat contracted and water blurred his vision.

"Oh, now you're gonna cry? You're a homo, aren't you?"

He ducked to avoid another slap to the face.

"Git out of my sight, you gay. I can't stand a gay."

Thankfully, his dream faded as another came to the front.

Something was whining, no squealing. He didn't realize what it was until he could see. The vision became clear and he saw a puppy in a small dog crate. The puppy shook like it was cold. The boy held the cage over a small pond of water. In an instant, he pushed it completely under water and watched as the puppy struggled to get out. He pulled the crate out of the water and the puppy blew water from his noise and began barking and yapping loudly. He laughed and dunked the crate again.

This time the puppy was coughing and sneezing when he pulled the crate from the murky water. He laughed again at how helpless the little dog was. He

felt good—powerful.
  He pushed the crate down again.

Scott opened his eyes, wide awake. He lay in a small bed in a little bedroom. The pillow was soaked in sweat. A chest of drawers stood in the corner. He saw a small window high up on one wall. Climbing on the bed, he looked through the window. A wooden privacy fence blocked most of his view. Beyond the fence, another house and then another and another spread out into the distance.

Two doors exited the room. One was open. It led to a bathroom. The other was closed. He tried to open it, but it was locked. Someone had turned the locking mechanism around so the lock could be activated outside the bedroom.

The visions Scott had read had unnerved him. As in all of the visions, Scott felt he was doing them, living them as he read them. Yet, these were so perverse it made him sick to think he may have experienced them.

He pounded on the door. It opened, almost instantly. A short, squat young man with thick buck teeth, thick glasses, and a stringy goatee came inside and said, "Sit on the bed." The size of his teeth gave his words a light lisp.

Scott did as he was told, realizing the visions he just had were from the guy standing in the doorway.

"Are you feeling all right?" Bucky asked. "The medication you received is…"

Scott interrupted. "Where's Blackwell?"

"He's making arrangements."

"Where am I?"

"Can't tell you," Bucky answered.

"Who are you?" He could call him "Bucky" but he thought that might not be a good idea.

"Yeah, you're feeling fine. And Dr. Blackwell's right. You ask too many questions."

"So what's your name?" Scott asked.

Bucky paused for a moment and ran stubby fingers through his goatee hair. "Kyle," he said. "Call me Kyle."

"When will Blackwell get back?"

"Soon." Kyle snickered and closed the bedroom door behind him.

***

"Hello, Scott. Did you have a nice nap?" Blackwell said when he marched into the bedroom about an hour later. Creepy Kyle followed him and stood guard by the door. "Kyle told me you were awake. Wonderful."

Scott sat up on the bed. The little bedroom was beginning to remind him of the jail cell he had been in after he read Jeff Gray.

"Here's the deal," Blackwell said, pacing back and forth before Scott. His pacing, impeded by his injury at the cross-walk, was awkward and slow. "You will have the ability to use this room, your bathroom, the living room outside this door, on occasion, and the kitchen. The other rooms of the house are out of bounds. You cannot leave this house unless I take you outside. Is that clear?"

"I know how it goes," Scott said. "If I try to escape, you'll kill my dog."

"Oh, no," Blackwell said. "Kyle, here, has your address. He will kill your dog." Kyle grinned from the doorway, looking like an evil Bugs Bunny.

Scott had a quick mental snapshot of the boy killing the puppy. He didn't want this wacko anywhere near another living creature.

"Then he will kill your wife," Blackwell added.

Scott felt his fists squeeze tightly by his side.

"Come into the living room where we can talk comfortably," Blackwell said.

Scott followed the odd pair through the doors. The living room was furnished in Early American Goodwill, apparently several years and several tenants ago. Dingy curtains clung to the sides of a big picture window. Blinds prevented them from seeing anything beyond the house.

A recliner sat across from the sofa. A small TV occupied a corner of the room, tethered to a video game console. The walls were bare. The kitchen was much smaller than the small one in Scott's house. A microwave oven sat next to a toaster oven on the counter. An aging refrigerator groaned beside an oven splattered with grease stains. Otherwise, the kitchen was empty.

"Tonight, we have access to an MRI lab at a nearby university," Blackwell explained. "All three of us will go there and we will get some complete scans of your brain. We'll also have blood drawn. Finally, I hope to have time for some basic X-rays of your skull," he said, almost sounding giddy.

Scott didn't like the thought that Blackwell might poke around in his brain and he shivered to think Kyle might be helping him, but realized if they were preoccupied with him, they couldn't bother Grace.

"You will be blindfolded whenever you leave the house with us. The less you know about where you are, the safer we all are, don't you agree?"

Scott wasn't sure if he did.

"After all of our tests are over, we won't bother you again. You will be able to go about your life as if you never met me," he added. "It's going to be a long night, so you may want to take advantage of the remaining hours this afternoon to get some sleep," Blackwell said.

Scott returned to the room. He heard Blackwell lock the door from the outside. Someone, probably Kyle, flipped on the television in the other room. Within a moment loud explosions, gunfire and recorded voices alerted Scott that Kyle must be playing some first-shooter video game.

He let the noise fade away and allowed himself to rest. He couldn't sleep. He didn't know if he'd ever be able to sleep again.

***

Several hours later, Scott was blindfolded and hooded and walked to the car. After about an hour, the car came to a stop and he was dragged inside a building. Once inside, the covering was removed and he squinted at the bright overhead lights. As soon as his eyes had adjusted, he searched for information—anything; documentation, logos, t-shirts—to reveal the name or location of the lab they were in. He assumed they were in a university.

234

A wooden door to one side opened and a bald man with a large cranium that looked out of proportion to his thin body entered the room. He smiled a hideous, toothy grin and welcomed Blackwell to the facility. Neither man offered to shake hands, but the skinny man leaned in to talk quietly with Blackwell.

"This is Dr. Gartside," Blackwell announced, "a noted neurosurgeon here at this university. He will be helping us with our work."

"Dr. Grimm," Scott mumbled.

The weird old man keyed a number into a keypad beside a metal door and the four men slipped inside. Fluorescent lights switched and flickered on overhead, illuminating the sanitary room. Scott changed into a hospital gown and sat in an armless chair where Blackwell extracted some blood. Dr. Gartside gathered several pieces of equipment from various cabinets and drawers and placed them on a stainless steel cart. Kyle stood in one corner and watched.

"Dr. Gartside will run some tests on the blood while we proceed with our examination," Blackwell said. "I'd rather not have to rent this room more often than I need to. It's quite expensive." Dr. Gartside looked up with the same creepy grin. Blackwell must have provided a sizable bribe for the use of this facility.

"Tonight, I'd like to get some baseline images of your brain activity. We will start with a Magnetoencephalography examination." He said the word in a tone of arrogance, as if only he and Dr. Gartside would understand. He was right. He led Scott into another sterile room that contained a strange, cream-colored device that looked somewhat like the tube on a park waterslide. It opened to an unusually long bed on rollers. Scott laid on the bed and Blackwell used a pen-shaped tool to stroke the area around his head, explaining this procedure provided a roadmap of his brain which the computer would use to guide the test. He gave Scott a pill of Alprazolam, and said, "In a moment I'm going to want you to read Kyle. This equipment will help me understand which portions of your brain work as you receive your readings."

At that point, Scott realized that the doctor's information about his trip with Grace was limited. He knew they were away, but apparently didn't know that Scott had the ability to read people without medication. He tucked this information away in case he might need to use it later.

Blackwell added, "I will be behind the glass window in that room while we perform this test. It is important that you remain perfectly still so we can collect accurate data."

Scott lay still, as instructed, while Kyle rolled his bed inside the tube. He thought of Grace and the agony she must be enduring, not knowing where he was or if he was safe.

"All right," Blackwell's voice boomed over the intercom. "We are ready to begin. Scott, I want you to relax and allow yourself to read my assistant, Kyle."

He did as he was told. He had perceived the three individuals and started to move close to one when a searing pain burned between his ears. He screamed.

236

He tried to sit up but the device covered the top part of his forehead and he couldn't pull his head out. "Stop! Make it stop!"

Blackwell, followed by the bumbling Kyle, rushed into the room. Kyle pulled the bed back and Blackwell moved close to Scott's head. In his haste, he had failed to replace his dark glasses, revealing the hideous orifice that once was an eye.

"What did you do?" Scott asked. "You had it up too high."

"There is no 'high' setting on the device, you idiot," Blackwell said. He moved around to the side of the bed and his eyes drew wide. "Get me the first-aid kit." Kyle left the room and returned with a white plastic box containing the bright Red Cross logo. He also brought in Blackwell's glasses

"What happened? What's going on?" Scott asked.

Blackwell wiped some ooze from his cheek and slipped the glasses on. "You've had a little fissure open up. It's nothing to be concerned about." He dabbed an anesthetically treated pad of gauze to Scott's neck just below his ears. "There, that's better," he said.

Dr. Gartside entered the room and inspected the tunnel at the base of the device. He used a white cloth to rub the headrest. Scott turned his head to see a crimson liquid on the cloth. "What the hell?" He placed his right hand to his ear lobe and pulled away bloody fingers. "What have you done to me?"

"Apparently, there was a reaction to the magnetic impulse produced by the MEG device. Obviously, whatever gives you the ability to read visions is ultra-sensitive to magnetic fields. We won't be using devices like this anymore."

"We won't be using any devices anymore," Scott said. "I'm out. My head feels like it was squeezed in an electric vise. Jesus! You tased my brain. I don't want anything to do with this."

"Now, calm down," Blackwell said. "We'll use less invasive techniques and take it slowly. If you have any pain, we'll stop the procedure immediately."

"Did you subject my twin brother to this study?"

Blackwell's demeanor changed from apologetic to irritation. "Why, yes we did," he answered matter-of-factly. "I had to find out if you had the same response. It was really a short burst."

"You son of a bitch," Scott fumed. "You knew what was going to happen and you still did it."

"All in the name of science."

"Science, my ass. You could have fried my brain."

"I didn't."

The two men glared, waiting for the other to blink.

Blackwell broke the silence. "Let us continue with our research."

"No deal," Scott said. "I'm not going to do this shit."

"You don't have a choice," Blackwell said, facing Scott. "Just give me a reason…"

"I know, you'll have Kyle drive back to my house."

"Yes, and he will wake your sleeping wife," he threatened again.

Scott looked at Kyle.

He smiled a gruesome grin that made Scott dread him even more.

"We must be careful with these tests," Dr. Gartside said, stroking the outside of the device. "This is extremely delicate equipment."

Blackwell ignored the remark and instructed Kyle to help Scott off the bed. Scott followed him to the control room and eased down carefully into a comfortable chair.

"Go help Gartside clean the machine," Blackwell barked at Kyle and the assistant went back into the room with some paper towels and cleaning spray.

Scott had just learned another piece of important information. It must be past midnight back home. Blackwell threatened that Kyle would 'wake up' Grace. Assuming she normally awoke at six or seven in the morning, Scott figured she was less than five hours away by car. It wasn't much, but he would take any information he could get.

"Obviously the MEG scan did not work, so we will try a couple of other non-invasive experiments while we still have access to these facilities." He started with an EEG test, which used sensing devices placed on Scott's scalp. He had to scrape tiny areas in Scott's skin to attach the conducting pads.

"Jesus," Scott said, ducking his head. "You call this, 'non-invasive'?"

The test lasted almost an hour, during which Scott was videotaped and asked several questions and, at times, shown a tiny, flashing light.

Scott was given other tests throughout the night

using various machines, and began to wonder if the tests themselves might kill him. At any rate, he didn't want to take any more. He'd been poked and probed and questioned 'til he hurt all over. His brain had been subjected to magnetic waves, light, electricity, radiation, and other sources he never knew existed. More than anything he wanted to go back to the house and rest. "Can we go now?" he insisted.

Blackwell nodded. They straightened the lab materials and prepared to leave. Dr. Gartside stayed behind to enter information into a computer.

Scott welcomed the blindfold. They were leaving.

***

The next morning, Scott entered the kitchen hoping to find breakfast—bagels, cereal, anything. Instead, laptop computers, reams of printed documents, and thick hardback books filled every empty space in the kitchen and dining room. Like a bottom feeder, Blackwell first scooped up this information from that source and then that information from another source. Kyle was busy doing assignments on demand, as Blackwell called them out. "Print that report," "Look up this drug," and, "Tell me where that source was?"

Scott got the feeling that was how Blackwell "earned" his doctorate in the first place—by focusing solely on the subject and farming out the grunt work to undergraduate students.

"Do we have any breakfast?" he asked no one in

particular.

"Peanut butter and jelly sandwiches," Kyle called from behind a laptop screen. "By the fridge."

Scott slapped some smooth peanut butter onto the side of a white slice of bread and married it with another slice. He also found milk in the refrigerator and helped himself to a glass. Across the room the television silently played a broadcast of a regional news station. His photograph filled the screen and, "Missing" appeared above the picture. Beneath it, words announced a reward would be given to anyone with information about the whereabouts of Scott Moore.

He had seen reports like this throughout his life. Some announced nefarious characters who had absconded with something valuable—money, paintings and worse, children. Others declared innocent individuals who had vanished as Ray Sawyer had in the mountains. Sometimes the missing people were never found. More often than not, they did manage to eventually turn up. As Scott hoped he would.

Blackwell noticed Scott was staring at the television. He snapped to Kyle, "Turn that damn thing off." The screen went blank.

"What we have done," Blackwell said, turning back to Scott. "We've analyzed your blood to determine what is in there besides, well, blood. Then we compared the parts of your brain that produce some of the chemicals and endorphins that exist in your blood to try to understand how your brain enables those psychic capabilities. We've also attempted to locate the source of your ability. It appears to be primarily in the cortex, of course."

"Of course."

"Then, we can reverse-engineer this, using some documents I found from Dr. Dekhtyar's original works that will help confirm our notion to create our own psychic-producing formula."

"Good. So when can I go home?"

"Mr. Moore. If all goes well, we will return you to your home within a few days."

Scott didn't put much stock in Blackwell's estimates. He wondered if he would ever get home. Munching on his peanut butter sandwich, he recalled the vision he had had of he and Grace in the mountains, worried that it might be another false vision.

CHAPTER EIGHTEEN

That afternoon, Scott was confined to his room when someone knocked on the front door. Now he knew how Gumby must have felt, locked away from anything and everything that was happening just belong the door. He tried to listen to the conversation in the other room, but the voices were soft and muffled. Sitting on the bed, back to the wall, he allowed his mind to wander. His wife…his work…his dog…

The silly brown boxer had brought such spontaneous happiness to their lives. It was amazing how simple activities seemed to be the most fun: chasing a Frisbee, swimming in a mountain lake, lounging by a fire, trying to catch a squirrel. Gumby had filled a gap for them, left by Scott's inability to have kids. Other parents nurtured children, went to parent meetings, baseball games and school plays, but Scott and Grace only had Gumby. Sitting alone in the gloomy room, he wondered if he would ever see the floppy-eared mutt again.

"Get the fuck out!" Blackwell's voice boomed

loud and clear through the thin walls. "All of you. Get out! You're no good. You've failed. Get the fuck out of this house!"

Blackwell must have been testing his "psychic drug" on various volunteers, obviously without success. He tried to read the people from his bedroom, but they left too quickly, with a violent slam of the front door.

Scott tried the door to his room but found it was locked. He pounded on it. "Let me out," he yelled.

It opened to an irritated looking Kyle.

"What's going on?" Scott demanded.

"Nothing," Kyle said. "We tried it and it didn't work."

"Good. So we leave now?" Scott asked, knowing the answer.

"You'll leave when I say you can leave," Blackwell yelled from the other side of the room. He was staring intently at a laptop screen. "There are other things we can do. We may need to take extreme measures."

His words made Scott a bit queasy.

"You'll learn," Kyle said. "He doesn't give up very easily."

***

Blackwell's recent failure and the verbal explosion that followed caused Scott to worry about what might happen if Blackwell ultimately failed in his efforts to replicate Scott's ability. He might take it out on Scott, by killing him and perhaps Grace, too. Scott told himself such insane thoughts were

244

nonsensical. Blackwell would have no logical reason to hurt her. But then, Blackwell wasn't logical.

Kyle's words kept banging about in his skull. "He doesn't give up easily." Trite. Simplistic. But hidden deep within the five-word sentence lay a truth Scott knew very well. Blackwell would not give up. He was pit-bull determined. He would never let go. Blackwell had persevered even after killing his first subject, Scott's twin, somewhere in Pennsylvania. He had hunted Scott down like a bounty hunter chasing a criminal. He had somehow survived a brutal hit-and-run accident right before Scott's eyes. Now he was on the verge of duplicating Scott's gift—his secret. Blackwell didn't give up easily. He would stop at nothing to profit from his tireless efforts. Nothing! Scott and Grace would be speed bumps in Blackwell's race for wealth and fame. If they got in his way, Scott had no doubt he would do away with both of them without thinking twice.

Scott had few alternatives. Either escape or die trying.

That night, he excused himself following an early dinner. The swirling thoughts, the non-stop noise, and his own fears drove him to search for a solution. He had to get away. For Grace. For himself.

Before entering the room, he paused quietly just inside the doorway. Taking a couple of dimes he'd had in his pocket when he was kidnapped, he pressed them, one by one, into the hole behind the strike plate in the door jam. If he could block this small hole he hoped the latch assembly would not slide through the strike plate, allowing him to open the door, even if it was locked from the outside. It had worked when he was a kid and wanted to sneak out late at night to hang with his friends. Hopefully it would work now. It was a long shot, but it was a shot.

Darkness devoured the day and with the waning light, he became more nervous. He sat on the edge of the bed, tapping his foot against the floor. The move he was about to take, if he followed through, might be his last.

Eventually, Scott heard the sounds in the other room proceed as they had the night before. Blackwell wrapped up his studies after slamming a massive textbook closed. In the background, a printer could be heard spitting out reams of paper for the next day. Scott heard footsteps on the linoleum floor in the kitchen as Blackwell plodded back to his bedroom at the other end of the house.

Then Kyle went into action. The lights beneath Scott's bedroom door dimmed as he turned off most of the lights in the family room and the sound of the television, muffled a bit, seeped through the walls. First, he heard the rhythmic pounding of shootout gunfire in a violent personal shooter video game. Then, the sound stopped, followed by the undeniable soundtrack of cheap porn, with the same sixteen bars of sleazy music repeated over and over and punctuated by guttural moans and sighs of fake passion.

He searched the room for a weapon he could use to disable the watchman but the tiny room was almost bare. The small, plastic trashcan in the corner would do no harm. The heavy dresser was too cumbersome. Old coat hangers in the closet were useless, even for hanging clothes.

He lifted the mattress on the bed to find the only make-shift weapon in the room—bed slats. He pulled one out and inspected it. Made of thin wood, about an inch thick and three inches wide, it might be used to strike an opponent, but it required that he get within three feet of his adversary.

Ultimately, Scott wasn't sure he could wield the weapon with the force that would be necessary to disable Kyle. He had never been violent. Even in this hopeless situation he didn't know if he could stop the guy he used to call Bucky. But he had to try.

Within time, the noise from the television ended. He heard Kyle rustling with the sofa bed as he set it up for the night. Finally, a not-so-soft snoring sound came from the room, indicating he had fallen asleep.

Taking his weapon in his left hand, Scott tiptoed lightly to the bedroom door. Carefully, he placed his hand on the doorknob, twisted it a little to the right, and gently pulled it toward him. As he had hoped, the door slid open noiselessly. Crouching down onto his haunches he crept toward the back of the house. His time in this tiny prison had done little to prepare him for maneuvering to the back door through the dark. Chairs he had seen time and again in daylight somehow blocked his path. A table holding computers, monitors and printers seemed to have moved in the night and now appeared as a dangerous obstacle. Gingerly, he picked his way through the darkness and sought the back door, the backyard, and freedom.

Eventually, he reached the gateway to escape. He feared the sliding glass door would be difficult to open and it was. Pulling it to the left, it made a grinding sound as it rumbled partway open.

The snoring stopped.

Scott froze.

A big hulk shuffled about in the creaky sofa bed. "Uhhh," Kyle moaned, raising his head to squint into the dark. After a few tense moments he dropped his big melon back onto the pillow.

Scott realized he had been holding his breath. He exhaled as quietly as he could.

Setting the piece of wood down, he placed his foot into the space between the partially open door and the doorjamb and his hands on the door handle and he pushed the glass door. It was stuck. He pushed harder, but it wouldn't budge.

Sliding his shoulder into the gap for leverage, he pushed harder and the obstacle slid open with a horrible screech.

"Hey!" Kyle shouted from the sofa bed where he was now sitting. "What's going on?"

Scott grabbed the bed slat from where he had leaned it against the wall and charged the drowsing giant. He took two steps across the living room floor, shifting the wooden stick to his right hand. On his third step, he raised the make-shift club over his shoulder and twisted at the waist, prepared to strike. On step number four he swung for the cheap seats.

The flimsy bat caught Kyle somewhere in his forehead—Scott couldn't be sure in the dark. The bed slat shattered in the middle between Kyle's head and Scott's hands, but not before inflicting some real pain and damage.

Kyle's body flew backwards toward the other side of the sofa. However, he was only stunned. He rolled onto his side, holding his head, groaning, and muttering every curse word in the book.

Scott didn't wait to hear him out. Dropping what was left of the shattered bed slat, he pivoted and dashed for the partially open glass door. He slid through with little trouble and ran across the concrete patio and into the backyard.

And, for a second, he froze again.

***

Scott had never been in the backyard. He had glimpsed it a few times as his captors entered or left the house, but generally, any view of the yard was covered by vertical blinds.

Surveying the area quickly, he saw that it was completely enclosed by a six-foot privacy fence. The space was devoid of trees, giving it a naked, dead look. The dim light from a half-moon, concealed a bit by gray clouds, only made it seem more dreadful, casting shadows here and there.

He had three options. He could run to the left or right sides of the yard and climb the fence, but then he would be closer to his pursuers were they to run around the outside of the fence. He chose the third option and ran as fast as he could to the back of the yard.

He leapt for the fence. For a second, he thought he had jumped too soon, misled by the dim light, but his fingers closed around the top edge and his right foot hit one of the crossbars. The old fence sagged outward, as if it was going to fall over and collapse in a heap on the other side, but then it slowly bounced back into position. Using his arms and his right foot, he flung himself over the top.

At that point he realized he had no idea what was on the other side of the fence. He might be jumping into a pond full of snakes, or a briar bush, or a yard of Dobermans. But the landing was without incident. He hit the hard ground, did a shoulder-roll, and kept running.

This second yard was not fenced. He sprinted by the small house and across the street in front of it. As he passed the driveway he caught a glimpse of Blackwell's BMW heading down the street that ran parallel to his path. He veered right through that yard and the next, trying to put some distance between himself and the black car.

And then he ran out of houses. The subdivision dead-ended onto a large, naked area of power transformers linked together by heavy cables. Giant towers tethered to one another flowed out in opposite directions from the transformers.

Scott searched for a way through the area, but it was surrounded by a high fence which was topped with several strands of barbed wire. A low drainage ditch ran between the road and the fence. He resumed his sprint along the road, trying desperately to get away from the two men chasing him.

A car suddenly turned the corner behind him and, with a thundering roar, sped in his direction. Scott somehow found the energy to run faster. As the car neared, he threw himself down into the ditch to hide. Crawling forward, he found a water culvert running beneath the road. Frightened as he was by what might be living in the culvert, he was more frightened by the two men in the BMW heading his way. He lunged headfirst into the dark, watery hole. Small creatures dashed ahead of him in the water, obviously scared of this monster that had invaded their home. He pressed on.

Overhead, he heard the BMW slow down and creep along the side of the road. They were obviously looking for Scott in the ditch. He hurried through the pipe until it opened on the opposite side.

Hugging the ground on the edge of the drainage ditch, Scott headed back up the road in the direction in which they had come. Hopefully, by the time they discovered the culvert, he would have slipped away.

Kyle's voice broke through the sounds of crickets and night creatures, "There he is! On the other side of the road."

The BMW made a U-turn and bright high beams shown in his direction.

Scott started to run again when Blackwell yelled, "We've caught up to you, Mr. Moore. Won't you come back quietly so we won't have to hurt you or your lovely wife?"

Scott stopped running.

Blackwell exited the car and came to where Scott

stood, hands on knees, sucking down breaths of air. In a moment, Kyle joined him. "Where the hell did you think you were going to go?" Blackwell asked.

Scott couldn't say anything. He simply leaned over further, still trying to catch his breath.

Off in the distance, another set of headlights turned onto the road and headed in their direction. All three men watched the car come toward them. When it was still a ways off, bright blue and red halogen lights on top of the vehicle began to flash, stinging Scott's eyes.

"Oh, shit," muttered Kyle.

The police car eased to a stop about fifty feet in front of Blackwell's BMW. A lone policeman stepped out of the car, hand on the gun in his holster.

"What are you boys doing out here?" he asked.

"Nothing to be concerned about," Blackwell said.

"Let me determine that," the officer said. "Now what are you up to?"

"Simply a domestic squabble," Blackwell said.

"I'll need to see some identification," the officer said, walking toward the three men.

"No problem, officer," Blackwell said, reaching behind himself as if to get his wallet.

"Officer, these men have kidnapped me. I need help," Scott yelled.

The policeman stopped, planted both feet on the ground and reached for his revolver.

With that, Blackwell whipped out a pistol from the waistband of his pants, pointed it at the officer, and pulled the trigger twice.

He flew back onto the hard, rough asphalt.

Scott stumbled backwards and down into the ditch.

"Now look what you've made me do," Blackwell accused. "Damn you, Mr. Moore." He pointed the gun directly at Scott.

Scott stared back, wide-eyed.

Blackwell tilted his head slightly. "Why don't you go back to my car, or would you like to share the fate of this police officer?"

Scott climbed back up out of the ditch. "You can't kill me. Not until you have perfected the process."

Blackwell scratched the back of his head and seemed to ponder Scott's remarks for a moment. Then he turned to his partner. "Kyle, see that he gets in the car. Remember, it's your fault that he got away."

"Yes, sir," Kyle muttered. He climbed down into the ditch and grabbed Scott's arms, perhaps a bit more tightly than was necessary, and pushed him toward the BMW.

Blackwell walked over to the police officer's body and double-checked it to make sure he was dead. He fired two more bullets into it, turned and walked nonchalantly to the car. The three men headed back to the house.

Scott slept behind a locked door blocked by a large recliner that night. It seemed as if all of his options were now locked away.

***

Blackwell began early the next day, demanding test after test. Scott complied reluctantly. He was probed and prodded. Blood was drawn and urine sampled again and again. Hours ran together like paint blended in a can, eventually turning into a nondescript, dark mess.

Since trying to escape the night before, he sensed the intensity of the study had risen several notches. Time was short.

Around seven o'clock that evening, he heard the front door open. Blackwell was talking with the visitor. After a moment, Scott recognized the voice as that of Dr. Grimm—Dr. Gartside. Something inside, another unusual sense, a feeling, a fear, swirled the bile in his stomach like scum ripples in pond water. This wasn't good.

"Scott! Join us in here," Blackwell boomed.

Scott emerged from his room to see the two men standing together near the kitchen table. Kyle stood closer to Scott's bedroom, looking as awkward as a seventh grader at his first school dance.

"I asked Dr. Gartside to come by so we could properly show our appreciation for his help." The skinny scientist grinned his creepy grin and clasped his hands behind his back. Together, the two could have been comfortable in an old black-and-white horror movie—the mad scientist and his assistant. Behind them some sort of leather and wooden contraption leaned against the wall.

The whole event smelled like shit. It didn't fit within Blackwell's standard operating procedure. Dr. Gartside looked nervous and Kyle looked like he might wet his pants. Something was happening and it wasn't good.

"I thought we should celebrate our partnership."

Scott shuddered to consider the various meanings of Blackwell's words. "I don't understand."

"Imminent success!" Blackwell proclaimed. "We have made such strides since you joined us Scott, we need to celebrate." He held up a bottle of champagne. Four flutes stood in line like soldiers, face down on the table.

Scott knew Blackwell had no use for him if he had duplicated the procedure and wondered if the bubbly might be poisoned. "If it's all the same to you, I'd just as soon head for home. It's been a long time…"

"Nonsense," Blackwell said. "First, we celebrate."

"No offense," Scott added. "It really would be nice to get home." While the words slipped from his lips, Scott sensed in the bottom of his gut that Blackwell had no plans to take him home.

He countered, "Scott, I know this ordeal has been tough and I am so very sorry that we had to use such archaic methods to persuade you to help. Please understand that this has been my life's work. And since the accident, I've had to take drastic measures. Let's face it. It's going to take a lot of plastic surgery before they will let me teach a university class." He stood in the middle of the room looking like a sad puppy with his drooping eye socket and scarred face. "Let's share some champagne and then we'll take you home, Scott." He grinned a sleezy used car salesman's grin.

Kyle, who had entered the bedroom while Blackwell was making his pitch, came out with Scott's overnight case and placed it by the door as if trying to prove the celebration was real. He placed a firm hand on Scott's shoulder and guided him toward the kitchen table.

Scott reached out to shake Gartside's hand, saying, "Thank you for joining us," as politely as he could. Talk around the table was light as Dr. Blackwell popped the cork. He seemed to stare at Scott with his one good eye.

Scott had to take advantage of this time to learn as much as he could about his three adversaries around the table. His life, and Grace's, probably depended on it. He could read Blackwell and Kyle again, but he knew all about them. However, he knew virtually nothing about Dr. Gartside other than that he had access to some fancy equipment. He worked hard to make himself relax without showing it. To the others in the room he had to appear to be paying close attention. His sole advantage was that Blackwell and the others had no idea he could read on demand. Taking a deep breath, he saw the images of the three men standing around the table. He moved straight into Dr. Gartside's vision.

The clatter about the kitchen faded away, replaced by the loud applause of an enthusiastic audience. As skinny Dr. Gartside, he stepped onto the stage and shook hands with the man at the podium who handed him a handsome plaque.

He slipped from that vision and into another and immediately jumped back, startled.

He was in a car accident. The car he drove rolled side-over-side only to be stopped when it wrapped around a huge tree. His right knee screamed in pain and he was trapped in the mangled car. Looking at his leg, he saw a jagged bone and something white protruding from his bloodied leg.

Blackwell interrupted his voyeuristic activity, "Join us, everyone." He flipped one of the champagne flutes over and poured in the golden effervescent liquid. Ceremoniously, he filled the next and the next until all were ready. Each person retrieved one of the thin glasses.

Scott lowered his guard a bit, knowing they were all drinking from the same bottle that had been sealed just moments ago. "First, thank you Dr. Gartside, for assisting us and for allowing us to use your wonderful facility at the University…at the university." He stopped the toast there and smiled, as if preventing himself from releasing the school name.

Scott feared Blackwell was about to kill him, so it seemed odd that he might hesitate to release the university name. But Blackwell's continued toast brought him back to his senses. "And let is thank you, Mr. Moore." He raised his flute and the others mimicked him. "Thank you, Scott. Because of the breakthroughs we will shortly accomplish, others in our country, in our world, will share your marvelous gift."

Scott slipped partially out of his trance wondering if the world was ready for such a "gift."

He tried to ignore Blackwell so he could finish his reading of Dr. Gartside, but Blackwell kept talking.

"Imagine…," he said.

***

"Imagine the opportunities. The military applications alone are worth billions. We will know the enemy's plans five moves before they know them. Corporations that are willing to pay for our services will out-compete and out-produce those who refuse to participate. Hell, in your field of Human Resources, Scott, forget background checks. One recruiter, properly trained and treated, will cull the good candidates from the bad and your hiring problems will go away. Poof!"

The idea of having a "properly trained and treated" staff made Scott cringe again. He had to escape. If he could run away now, he would. He would dash through the front door, sprint to the road in front of the house, choose a direction – left or right, and flee as fast as any man could run.

They would pursue him. He knew too much to think Blackwell would let him go. And they would catch him and they would kill him. Then, they would find Grace and kill her, too.

It seemed ironically odd that the man who could see the future had none himself.

Scott had never feared death. He assumed he was

ready for whatever was after life. But now, so close to his own demise, he realized he was not ready. He had too much to do. Death would bring too many regrets.

And, behind his fears and misgivings was Grace. He had to do whatever he could to protect her. How?

He was in a bad place, both figuratively and literally, and he saw no way out.

Blackwell called for a toast. "May our visions take us to places we've never been before."

His toast was odd and paradoxical. After all, Scott's gift had done exactly that. Time and again he went to places in the memories and visions of those he met, where he had never been before. He saw things he wasn't meant to see. He invaded people's lives without their knowledge of it and he brought back information he did not deserve to have. He was like a voyeur, standing outside a stranger's window.

The other three sipped their drinks in the afterglow of success. Scott found it difficult to drink the champagne, not because he thought it might be tainted—he had seen others drink from the same bottle, and the bottle had been sealed when Blackwell opened it. However, it was hard to put the glass to his lips. His hands were shaking so hard because he sensed his own death was coming soon.

He slipped back into a state of relaxation and focused on one of the last visions of Dr. Gartside.

As the doctor, he stood before a stainless steel cart containing several ominous looking instruments. He picked up one, a long glass tube, attached to an even longer, brass needle. He turned around and faced a leather and wooden table that stood nakedly in the middle of the living room. The table looked somewhat like one a masseuse might use, covered with leather and containing a large padded hole at one end. Looking more closely, Scott saw a man's body, strapped to the table on his stomach, with his face secured to the padded hole with a leather mask. His hands and feet were also clasped to the table with leather restraints. A video image overhead revealed an image not unlike the human brain.

Blackwell interrupted the vision. "Scott, you haven't touched your champagne."

Looking up, he realized everyone but he had taken a sip from their glasses. He pulled his flute to his lips and paused. "I was just thinking about Kyle." He halfway turned to face the strange man. "How's your old man? Do you miss him? How many times did he beat you?"

"What?" Kyle raised his face, revealing shocked and frightened eyes.

"You remember," he said, trying hard to divert everyone's attention to Kyle. "Did you begin to enjoy it when he slapped you around?"

Gartside didn't know what he was talking about, but started laughing an evil-sounding laugh at Kyle in his embarrassment.

Blackwell was beginning to piece together what was taking place. He said, "He's reading an episode from your past, Kyle." Then added, "But how can you do that without your medicine?" Suddenly, a knowing look passed over his face as if lit up by a searchlight.

"Is that why you killed that little puppy long ago?"

"Huh?"

"You know. You drowned a puppy in a dog crate. Did it squirm and squeal when you pushed it under water?"

"I…how did you know?"

"That's what I do," Scott said.

With nothing to lose, he slipped back into the vision of Gartside.

The doctor carried the needle device to the table where the body lay. It was shaking now, squirming, struggling against the straps, and trying to get free. Gartside placed the device at the base of the skull, pointing upwards parallel to the spine. Watching the video image, he gave the device a firm shove. It slid beneath the skin and slowly up along the brainstem, through the thalamus and into the cerebrum.

Pulling back on a ring like device at the other end of the tube, a murky white fluid slowly filled the tube.

He heard a terrifying wail from the body on the table and realized what he had suspected was true. The scream was his. He was the man lying on the table.

"No," he shouted, jolting alert. "You can't do this."

"Get him, you fools."

Kyle still looked stunned, but reached out to grab Scott. Gartside looked scared.

"Let me go," Scott yelled, and turned to sprint for the door. "You're all insane. You can't do this!"

"We have to," Blackwell said. "It's the only way…"

Kyle bear-hugged him from behind. Gartside began to set up the table.

Still holding the champagne flute in his hand, he squirmed, kicked, and elbowed Kyle, but the little giant would not let go. He half-carried, half-dragged him toward the table.

Gartside plunged a hypodermic into his shoulder, but Scott swatted at it with his left hand, knocking it away.

Dr. Blackwell shouted, "Be careful. Not too much. We don't want to pollute the cerebral fluid."

But some anesthesia did reach his system. Scott began to slip. He felt his body go weak. His arms and legs tingled. He couldn't let this happen; couldn't let them do this, couldn't die like this.

But he couldn't stop it.

***

Blackwell looked on as Gartside held him on the left and Kyle on the right.

Minimally sedated, Scott was dragged to the table. He could still think, reason, plan—just a little. But he didn't have much control of his body and he needed to get it back, somehow.

And the plan came to him. It was risky. It might

not work. But it was the only plan he could think of.

Holding the glass flute in his left hand, he smashed it on the table, shattering the glass and forcing shards into his palm. The painful shock fueled adrenaline waking him from his semi-stupor.

The move shocked Kyle, too, who loosened his grip just a bit. Little things mean a lot. A flash of clear thought, a desperate move, a loose grip, and big, important things can happen.

Scott grasped the stem of the glass with his bloody hand, gasping from the pain. He jerked his left hand with the glass stem over his right shoulder, catching Kyle in his neck.

Kyle sucked in air. He pulled the glass away, dropped it, and then clutched his bleeding neck, backing away. The wound didn't kill him, but it sure as hell surprised him.

Scott made his next move. He put all his weight on his right foot and raised his left knee as high as it would go. With a mighty force he thrust his foot directly at Gartside's right knee. He felt the cartilage pop as it gave way.

"Stop him," Blackwell shouted.

Scott dashed for the door and saw a set of keys on the table. He grabbed them and yanked the door open. Three cars were parked in the driveway: Blackwell's BMW, an older Volvo he assumed belonged to Gartside, and a Mustang—probably Kyle's. Clicking the remote FOB, he was glad to see the lights flash on and off on the Mustang. He didn't care for Volvos.

Somehow, Kyle stumbled through the door and lunged toward Scott. He made a swiping grab motion and managed to catch his left foot. However, he didn't have a firm hold, and the effort only served to trip Scott, who fell forward, tucked, and rolled through the gravel in the driveway. Pain shot through his arm and shoulder. He came up on his feet and dashed for the car.

Scott looked up to see Blackwell running through the doorway. "Get in the car, Kyle."

Gartside stayed inside, probably in intense pain.

Scott snatched open the Mustang door, driving pain into his left hand, and dove into the driver's seat. Cranking the engine, he felt it thunder to life. He jerked the gearshift to reverse and screamed out of the driveway. Then he pulled the lever into drive and jammed the gas pedal. The Mustang squealed out onto the street in a flurry of dirt, rocks, and smoke, barely missing Kyle, who lay on the ground, struggling to get up.

Scott was free!

***

He had no idea where he was. He didn't even know the name of the city, but he didn't have time to stop and ask.

Thundering down two-lane streets, past downtown shops and brick buildings, he searched desperately for something to help him know which way to go.

A sign flashed by pointing to Interstate 24. He turned onto the on ramp and flew north on the interstate highway and then forced himself to slow his mind down, lest he be pulled over by the police.

Then it occurred to him that the police may be the only people who could help him, so he would welcome seeing a blue light in his rear view mirror. He had no idea how he would explain that he was driving a stolen vehicle in an unknown town and trying to find directions home, but it just might work.

An exit sign zipped by. **'Nashville.'** He pounded the steering wheel with his right hand while holding onto the steering wheel with the fingers of his left hand to keep from pressing on the wound. He was in fucking Nashville, Tennessee. Now he knew where he was. If only he could figure out how to get home. Almost too late he realized he was heading in the wrong direction. He jerked the wheel over to the right and took the exit ramp. At the bottom of the ramp he turned left, dodging oncoming cars at the intersection, went under the interstate and headed left again to go back onto I-24 in the other direction. He floored it.

He weighed his options. If he had a cell phone, he could call Grace and have her meet him somewhere safe. They could run away together and stay away as long as necessary. He considered pulling off the highway to call from a pay phone, but pay phones are the dinosaurs of modern communication—there were few left. Also, he was sure Blackwell and Kyle were on their way to his house just as he was. If they got to Grace before he did, he knew they would kill her.

He could go straight to the police, but how would he explain his plight? The cops would never believe a mad doctor and his assistant were chasing him because he had psychic ability. They'd lock him up and destroy the key. And Grace would die.

As he left the Nashville city limits, the reality of his situation came back to him full force. He had just stabbed one man, broken another's knee, and staged a spectacular getaway. His hands began to shake uncontrollably. Fear wrapped around him like a boa and he almost started to cry. He shook off the fear. He had to make plans.

Scott searched Kyle's car. He was not surprised to find a pistol in the glove box. Flying down the highway at ninety miles an hour, he fiddled with the gun until he thought he had released the safety. He had to be sure. Pushing a button, he opened the moon roof overhead, pushed the gun out into the night sky and squeezed the trigger. The blast of the gun combined with the powerful recoil made him jump and jerk on the steering wheel, causing the racing car to zigzag back and forth. He jammed on his brakes and the car squealed and swerved until he regained control.

He was about four hours from home. It took him two and a half. No policemen came to his aid. At about one o'clock in the morning, he rocketed up the driveway and jammed the brakes to a stop. Grabbing the pistol he ran to the front door shouting at the top of his lungs, "Grace. Wake up. We've gotta get out of here."

Gumby charged the front door as he opened it, snarling, growling, and barking.

Grace ran out from the bedroom as he switched the lights on. "Scott!" She grabbed him in a full, welcome hug. "Oh, my God. I was so worried."

"No time. Grab some clothes. They may be right behind me."

"Who? What happened?"

"They were going to kill me after they discovered how to copy my ability," he said. "We'll talk about that on the road. Get dressed and come with me."

"Who?"

"Blackwell. He's still alive."

Horror filled her eyes with brutal blackness.

"Should I pack?"

"No time." He grabbed Gumby's leash and struggled to get the wriggling dog to stand still long enough to drape the leash over his neck.

Grace raced out of the bedroom wearing jeans and a sweatshirt. She grabbed her purse and headed for the door. "Should we take the Prius?" she asked.

"Hell, no."

"Where'd you get this?" she asked when they entered the driveway and saw the Mustang.

"You wouldn't believe me," Scott yelled. He opened the door, pulled the seat forward and half-lifted, half-pushed Gumby into the back.

Grace climbed in the passenger's side and Scott mounted the driver's. The engine roared and he shifted into reverse.

The rear of the Mustang jolted with a loud crash bouncing Grace and Scott from one side to the other. Gumby fared worse.

Blackwell's BMW collided with the left-rear side of their car, throwing the vehicle through the mailbox and into the front yard.

Scott's left hand exploded in pain as he squeezed

the steering wheel to stable himself. He quickly regained his senses and cranked the motor again. Jerking the wheel to the right, he aimed the car toward the street.

The passenger door of the BMW snapped open and Kyle jumped out just as Scott jammed on the accelerator. The Mustang hurtled forward, crushing Kyle and the door and pushing the BMW sideways.

Blackwell had pulled a shotgun from the back seat of the car. Somehow, he backed out of the driver's seat and away from the sliding vehicle. He aimed from the hip and pulled the trigger. The Mustang's rear tire ripped into shreds, tossing the car about like a rudderless ship in a violent storm.

Scott managed to pull the wheel around so the driver's side was facing Blackwell's car. He, too, jumped out of the car determined to stop this rampage or die trying. He aimed Kyle's pistol at Blackwell just as the doctor was reloading the shotgun. The bullet missed by inches. Blackwell raised the stock to his shoulder as Scott's second shot tore through the right side of his chest.

Blackwell was down, but not out. He was definitely at a disadvantage because his right eye was his good eye, but the right side of his body was now almost useless because of Scott's lucky shot. Still, he managed to tip the shotgun in Scott's direction and reach for the trigger.

Scott had taken five steps toward Blackwell and continued to march in his direction. He pulled the trigger on the pistol twice. The shots shattered the window in the BMW. He shot a fourth time and the bullet smashed into Blackwell's chest, hurling him back toward the ground.

Gumby barked furiously from the back seat of the Mustang.

Grace dashed around the front of the car to Scott who was checking to make sure Blackwell was dead. He extended his hand to the doctor's neck and felt for a pulse.

Blackwell's eyes opened wide and he gasped deeply. With a guttural groan, his eyes closed and his head fell back to the grass.

This time he truly was dead.

CHAPTER NINETEEN

The police surveyed the scene, roped off the cars with yellow tape, and asked a million questions. A young police officer identified himself as Officer Burton. He pulled out a notebook and sat opposite Scott and Grace in the living room where a paramedic had bandaged Scott's hand.

Scott was amazed at how calm he was. He proceeded to explain the situation as well as he could without saying anything about psychic abilities.

"Who were the two dead men in Scott's front yard?"

He said the two men had kidnapped him, thinking he was related to someone with lots of money, and held him against his will in Nashville. This fit well with Grace's earlier story when she reported Scott was missing.

"Who did they think Scott was?"

Scott had no idea. He said one guy kept calling him, "Luke."

"Does he know their names?"

Scott explained that they had not revealed much of their identities. Mr. Blackwell seemed to be the leader of the group. He didn't know Kyle's last name.

"What were they doing in Nashville? Could Scott find that location?"

They seemed to be manufacturing narcotics. They had lots of drugs and medicines around the house. Scott wasn't sure where the house was but they may be able to find it under Blackwell's name.

"Where did he get the Mustang?"

He explained that it belonged to Kyle and he had used it to escape. He drove straight to his home to prevent them from hurting Grace.

Grace listened intently to Scott's story and repeated it almost verbatim when she was questioned.

When the sun broke out through the morning clouds, the police collected their things and drove away.

Scott and Grace closed the front door and sat back down on the sofa. They were exhausted. Gumby was, too.

"Know what?" Scott asked his wife.

"What?"

"Officer Burton is going to have twins."

Grace chuckled and placed her head on his chest.

***

A few months later, Scott and Grace took Gumby to a nearby dog park. Several breeds of dogs frolicked in the large, fenced-in area. Gumby chased a Beagle around the park, his haunches tucked down low to the ground to gain speed.

Grace stayed in the fenced-in area and Scott took a walk around the trails that expanded out like tendrils to basketball courts, baseball diamonds, and skateboard ramps. He stopped about seventy-five yards away from the entrance of the park at a bench along the sidewalk.

A young girl, obviously pregnant, was sitting on another bench facing him. She wasn't wearing makeup and it gave her a harried, nervous look. It also made her look old. Her hair was a mess, as if she hadn't brushed it all day. The knees on her jeans were tattered and ripped. She clung to her purse as if it were the last thing she had in the world.

Scott asked softly, "May I ask you a personal question?"

She raised her head.

"When are you due?"

She sighed deeply. "About two more months," she said.

"Do you know what you'll have?"

"The doctor says it's a boy. Of course, he could be wrong."

Scott thought long and hard. "Yeah, I think the doctor's right." He spoke with the conviction of someone with knowledge.

"Guess I'll find out then."

"I have a pretty good feeling about these things," Scott said.

She was beginning to look irritated.

"You know, I think he's going to grow up to be a teacher."

"Fat chance," she said. "I ain't even finished high school. You think my son will be a teacher."

"No, you may be right. Not a teacher." He leaned forward. "A professor. He's going to teach at a big university."

"Ha, ha. Mister. You must be crazy."

"I've been told that before," Scott said. "But you know, sometimes the crazy people—the ones who dream dreams and see visions…sometimes, they know things."

The girl had a puzzled look on her face.

"Remember this," Scott said. "He's going to teach at a prestigious university." He leaned back on the bench and looked toward the dog park. Grace was standing at the gate watching him talk with the pregnant girl.

ABOUT THE AUTHOR

Tell stories." It's one of the best pieces of advice I've ever received. Stories inspire people to grow and expand their horizons. They entertain. They challenge. They comfort. Simply put, they make life much better.

I've been telling stories all my life. When I worked with youth years ago, I told stories that helped them understand, learn and develop. Later, as a corporate training manager I used stories to demonstrate examples, to encourage better business practices and to stimulate learning. As a college professor I found stories to be instrumental in challenging people to think and comprehend.

Today I continue to tell stories. You'll find them in my nonfiction curriculum books and all of my award–winning novels. My hope is you'll enjoy my stories and share them with your friends. Then, tell your own stories. It's a great piece of advice.

Facebook:
https://www.facebook.com/bsharp53

Twitter:
https://twitter.com/bsharpwriter

Website:
http://www.bensharpton.com/

I hope you've enjoyed 2nd Sight. You can help authors like me in several ways.

•Please tell your friends through word--of--mouth and social media.

•Sign up on the author's website to receive updates on new books and upcoming events.

•Provide feedback.

• Check out other books the author has written.

•Write an honest review of the book and post it on review sites, in blogs, on book sellers' sites, etc.

Thank you, in advance, for your help. I do appreciate it.